Generation Bloodbath

An early part of *Generation Bloodbath* appeared in
Ragged Lion Journal III (UK, May 2020)

Apocalypse Party

Design by Mike Corrao
Cover by Kier Cooke Sandvik

Paperback: 978-1-954899-76-6

Printed in the United States of America

FIRST AMERICAN EDITION

9 8 7 6 5 4 3 2 1

Generation Bloodbath

Paul Curran

PART 111

Black Sabbath

What is this that stands before me?

Figure in black which points at me

1

Before they burned the bodies, they performed several rituals unnoticed by anyone unfamiliar with new-regime iconography.

2

We wait for the trains bringing more bodies from inland to the boiling plants along the coast and clamber aboard to feed on whatever we find.

3

Cruelty's the wrong word for what I mean because, although what happened involved cruelty, the overriding atmosphere was one of headless pity.

4

The regime influenced my work in ways the regime only knew.

5

Independent reports confirm the impossibility of independent reports: the blood we smear across our lips distorts every utterance.

6

But the perfect picnic spot never took three years to reach, and in the hull of this ship, the rats feeding on us are closer to human.

7

It's difficult to write with one hand stabbing you in the face, but the vibrations from the jaw and the wrist make music, if that's your trip, and the blood and the blood and the blood and the blood and the blood and the blood and the blood and the blood.

8

If the regime moved into advertising, the world would be strewn with more corpses than was the field where we slept last night.

9

Traumatic incidents being more common than clean-up operations under the new regime, some bright kids arranged the masses of bodies into art.

10

The old regime, anticipating subliminal revolt, mixed ideology with a skin-absorbent coma-virus applied to toys in cereal boxes.

11

P: Take them away.
G: The pits are full.
P: Dig more.
G: The adults refuse.
P: Make the kids.
G: They're dead.
P: Give me a hug.

12

We sat half-buried in sand along the beach, chanting resistance slogans in the only language the new regime allowed, and our voices one by one drowned in wave after wave, as the tide rose on a beautifully simulated sunset created by various blood-stained mirror shards.

13

At night, the stairs to the ship's galley sound more brittle than whatever bones find themselves somehow under there, but this was never the darkest exit.

14

The last class of my new-regime course, Counteracting Downfall Narratives 101, was disrupted by a swarm of bees with stings containing morphine.

15

Hatred for the new regime paralyzed our ability to resist its presence, which was the reaction they expected, vanishing from our screams.

16

In a barn outside the firebombed city, we slept on hay soaked in so much blood it appeared blacker than red and spoke to us in occult jumbles.

17

We were told the new regime would heal the wounds within, but the words they used were worse than the wounds, and this was the bloodbath way.

18

Postmortem interviews with those who reportedly left through their own hands revealed an eccentric glossolalia corresponding with linguistic characteristics previously captured on mechanical phonograph cylinders launched into space before space was out there.

19

And on and on and on, and oh, yes, we've all heard your opinion of the Home Invasion Therapy (HIT) treatment for Generation Bloodbath.

20

The fleet burst into flames before we reached the reef, and the passengers died in ways they'd never expected, because their dreams were midnight assassin blunt traumas, but this was a flash of light, a synaptic trick, minor confusion leading to total panic, all against the narrative.

21

"Unwrite the horror of this world until there's nothing left" was the first, and the last, line of every old-regime novel ever written or unwritten.

22

New regime: We love you.
Old regime: We love you.
Neo regime: We love you.
Resistance: We love you.
Language: We love you.
Formula: We love you.

23

Plunging a knife into someone's neck is an intimate act, but the angle and the trajectory say more about your relationship to the attacked.

24

And the blood and the blood and the blood and the blood, gushing down to the stream where we clean our wounds with stems and storks, and before we can escape, the tanks are back, and any death is a good night's sleep, and the blood is our cult.

25

As usual, the kangaroo-court jury members were executed before the trial began, but their distorted voices were heard echoing after the judge passed sentence.

26

The last published interview with new-resistance leaders went unpublished because linguistic analysis revealed subtextual voices attacking the notion of leadership before culminating in meaningless babble of self-indulgent nonsense and/or hyper-violent threats aimed elsewhere.

27

In a sentimental turn, the new regime melted our wristwatches and railway tracks into far more brutal and effective torture devices.

28

The old regime reinvented reality to convince us we were ever free from the language battered into our DNA.

29

Attempts by the neo regime to persuade us they weren't a regime went from absurd to terrifying, a psychedelic bloodbath, within two minutes (jet packs for suicide belts).

30

They dragged us down our hallways and into our backrooms, although we were homeless, and shot us in our heads, although we were headless.

31

In this scene (series five, episode twelve: "Human Square"), set in a new-regime archive warehouse, calendar pages fall from walls and ignite, hitting floors collapsed under machines black and deep-red oiled and refined through linguistic-crime extraction procedures.

32

Endless imitation new-regime products assembled in post-regime death factories flood the market, barely sandbagged by our flabby resistance.

33

The old regime sells its codes to pharmaceutical detectives who transform them into a line of T-shirts with fiercer menace than the regime.

34

Exhausted from resisting the battle internal, we resigned ourselves to haunting the new regime through telepathic signals in pornographic magazines.

35

At least the adverts improved under the new regime, and we could pin our hopes to the stake-grim reality of impending extermination.

36

On the N-gram Sky Tower's sixty-sixth floor sits a scale model of a beach town, where pinpricks pepper regime hotels, and the sand is painted red.

37

Whatever's causing these convulsions and hemorrhaging must be contained not only in the bottles we drink but also in the words we use for water.

38

They torched the sleeping barn and made jewelry from our screams.

39

Post-regime life: a memory whose ghost haunts the millions involved in the slaughter of millions, and those related to the millions of slaughtered, and the millions of farmers chewing bones in blood fields circling the cities we used to call home and now call contagious.

40

Frantically drunk, our bottles half poison, we clamber for an exit, mice rattling gas-pipe cavities, unable to shake loose these shells.

41

We, the snow-globe shipwrecked, call upon the new-regime goons to alter the lighting above this sacrificial mantelpiece.

42

Or, remember trials implied mystery, but on TV-FUZZ, smashing heads against screens and crawling down hallways clinging to the truth is a lie?

43

The last dispatch from the resistance is a coded message calling on members to enter sleeper mode, and it's reported as mass suicide.

44

A: Are you coming with me?
T: I didn't book a ticket.
A: Where are you bleeding?
T: Don't touch.

45

A fierce wall of light comes over a hill, and the darkness explodes (pyrotechnics).

46

Generation Bloodbath is the end of time, the end of numbers, the end of generation, the end of regeneration, the end of degeneration, and the end of transcendence.

47

For a year or so, I couldn't remember my name or address, and although I continued to communicate, it was only with words written in the resistance manifesto's opening chapter.

48

I promise to stay hidden in the bulbous bow of this drunken space wreck.

49

The hallway features hand-knotted carpet on the floor and halfway up the walls, as well as a wood-paneled ceiling with glass chandeliers, and they grab me by the hair and drag me through the swinging doors, screaming: "Where's the cinema?"

50

Recruiting a bunch of kids to enact a school shooting made more sense when there were schools undemolished.

51

We were culled from neo-regime orphanages to feed the fashion for ritual abuse at shabby nightclubs in drunken seaside towns.

52

We walked through unending tunnels smelling of zinc, over unknown bodies mangled in upturned train carriages, and the more we walked, the less we were walking.

53

Pharmaceutical detectives followed us through cardboard

boxes, and station announcements came back at us in gray and white, cold water, closed.

54

I take no pleasure in killing (each murder leaves a mark, a trace, a scar, a scare).

55

The nerve cells I love do not exist in the speedboat loop of anyone with vision.

56

I asked the visitors what they wanted, and they said, "You don't resemble a suicide case," but they could have meant "assemble a suitcase" (for them, our language was fast food).

57

No Analysis: the only channel airing 24/7 live and recorded Atrocities (TV-FUZZ tagline).

58

The old-regime origin story (propaganda film), *A Picnic of Six*, features a faceless cabal, who are mysteriously drawn, independent of one another, to the same mountain-lookout suicide spot, where they meet each other and some blankets and change/destroy the world.

59

If this ship were a train, the slaughterhouse awaiting us would bloom flowers.

60

I want to eat your head, and your head wants to eat mine, so let's put them together.

61

I'm either too tired or don't care what happens next, but apathetic is how they want us to feel, so I strap the knife to my leg and dive into the river, and I sit on the bottom, and while waiting for you, I gaze up at the sunshine drifting through the bloody sediment.

62

Old-regime proverb: when the hammer comes down, no leg is left standing.

63

A telepathic blood transfusion is synonymous with swallowing blood.

64

I curl up on the riverbank and scribble desperate thoughts, inscriptions, carvings, and random coded sketches in the margins of a blood-soaked notebook, which has been dried and resoaked in different blood and redried and buried and unearthed.

65

Through the rope around my neck, I see you.

66

G: Stop. Wait there. Come back.

P: Don't be so childish. Get in the car.

Z: What do you want?

G: I have no control over my movements.

P: What's your name?

Z: You shouldn't have asked my age.

P: I'm not afraid of coming down.

67

I witnessed Armageddon through a telescope, from a time machine, in another dimension, and it was neither good nor bad, neither a whimper nor a bang, but my chest tightened, and a tear fogged the lens.

68

Our sincerity trapped the old regime into believing we came to fight.

69

The last to leave the planet allegedly lay frozen in rows.

70

Counting the dead was never an option.

71

The old regime might have disappeared, but the ghouls pouring from those festering tombs are infinitely more malignant.

72

Necro Solar Intercourse (NSI) became so popular that future burial beaches off the map were converted into training centers for new recruits to practice on corpses yet to expire.

73

Blood balloons float in the yellow sky above the city.

74

And I flip through photographic evidence—a person down the river this morning, an unsympathetic victim with a coat-hanger posture, the body contorted in ragged symmetry—but I'm unable to read the signs, and on the next slide, the person's an incinerated lump.

75

In with the radio, out with the birds.

76

The latest new-regime souvenirs include a plastic suffocation bag (jet packs for suicide belts) and a mass-produced icon of the Picnic of Six.

77

On the back of a truck at the airport, a wall of amplifiers emits a subsonic drone.

78

The wipers were melted to the white van's windshield, and on the dashboard sat a Walther P22, some drumsticks, and a snow globe.

79

Whenever I step off the platform, my shell shatters, or the train shatters (they say the old-regime goons broke less), but my soul, or whatever you call it, enters other bodies, and the bombs handle the rest.

80

I sit naked on a couch in a hotel room and stare at a painting on the wall ("Violent Sleep") and ignore the headless corpse beside me, and the torso on the bed, and the string dangling from a green balloon on the ceiling, and the blood and the blood and the blood and the blood.

81

New-regime undercover agents resemble old-regime undercover agents, difference taking a back seat in this space wreck to the stars.

82

And the gods have been gone for so many centuries, it means they were never here.

83

They selected whichever infants turned them on and led them to the captain's mess for hackneyed rape play and hacksaw games.

84

Unconfirmed reports might have said the blood was closer to nonhuman than human, but nonhuman blood never tasted this bitterly sweet (ketchup and corpse paint).

85

Our blood was precious to them, but to us it was poison in a bottle marked X.

86

The original *Backpackers Trashed by Axes* features three sets of friends who meet on a boat to an island where, one by one, backwards locals trash the friends with axes.

87

What the Blood Bath said: "For those about to hang, we collapse too."

88

A: Have you ever been in love?
T: What does love mean?
A: I used to cry for six hours after killing revolutionary resistance fighters.
T: You look familiar.
A: I had a face job and some ribs removed (oxygen fix).

89

The therapist/rapist makes a speech to the other inmates/ passengers/patients/subjects/stars about a suspicious new arrival, the dead leader's donkey-child.

90

The end came, and the end went, as the end comes and the end goes, and blood is thick etc., but have you ever woken up naked in a bathtub with the dismembered corpse of someone you vaguely remember sharing the sunrise with on the first day of New Regime Year Zero?

91

The demolished and polluted cities have been uninhabitable for so many years, the word for a collection of buildings in any location has vanished.

92

For example, we wanted to visit a cinema, but the cinema had disappeared, and the films it used to play had been destroyed, so we acted out various three-act structures with knives.

93

Beyond the knives, we dropped our reflections hoping for absence instead of a cracked skull.

94

The New Regime Intergalactic Headquarters (NRIH) not only demolished itself during construction but also while subliminal floor plans were being drafted and during initial meetings between departmental leaders and official architects soon shot dead.

95

We took our time unpacking, because we carried no luggage,

and the bomb craters were bigger than the swimming pools, but the blood and the water were the same.

96

The ships set sail, seven sturdy vessels, bow waves churning blood limb head torsos, sunset singing narcotic calm before night twitch ejaculations, and then come the ropes, the ropes, the ropes, the ropes, the ropes, the ropes, the ropes, the ropes, the burn.

97

The new regime retreated for the weekend, which landed once every six years, if anyone ever counted, allowing us to torture ourselves with our own lazy nightmares.

98

We walked and walked until what we were doing wasn't walking, or whatever we used to call walking, but soon we switched directions and found only flames.

99

Z: Are we dead as well?

G: Don't you love this place?

P: Tell me the first action you make in the morning?

Z: I fall.

G: Nothing to add.

100

Dear X, if you're reading this message, you found the bottle and opened the bottle and unfolded the paper and, in contrast to us, it hasn't perished, and the ink marks haven't been smudged into illegibility, in contrast to the stuff in our bodies when the hammer came down.

101

Passing the new-regime entrance exam is impossible because most questions are in a language without time, and blood carries a secret grammar.

102

For each Atrocity committed in the new-regime's name, those recorded in the Snuff Corpus, a million went unnoticed, and the infinite other possibilities unperformed carried enough weight to bleach the dreams from humanity.

103

Those sentimental old-regime dreams (e.g., murdered bedsheets or being hunted through shifting buildings and landscapes) scrape the gunk from my skullcap.

104

Phrases revealing our resistance to the regime's symbolic order are written on our burial T-shirts, and particularly the ones on fire never burn, never rot.

105

And the black rain comes down as the ship continues with its endless bloody churn.

106

In the cabin next to mine, unspoken violence comes and goes with the passing of light and/or, as they say, maybe love never broke my neck twice.

107

When the regimes were here and there, we knew roughly where or how we would die, but now we're left with these mouthy cult bullies nodding.

108

New-regime memory (74): the Ministry of Relocation calls to inform me that my family members have been relocated to a shallow pit near the beach.

109

As the call came through, I dropped my coffee, and all my other struggles fell away, the amphetamine pettiness and hope, with that new-regime voice.

110

A shadow falls across the entrance to the cave where we've been hiding, and soon we discover why the rabbits of the old regime have no ears.

111

In the early days, the days were early.

PART 222

War Pigs

Generals gathered in their masses

Just like witches at black masses

112

St. Regime appears on one side of a soggy playing card, and on the other side a lawnmower hovers across a bloodbath of severed hands and feet.

113

Nonsense suggesting the visitors infected the planet with microbes is the nervous laughter accompanying cracked skulls rubbing on undeveloped crotches in garbage-lined alleyways outside ruined buildings, where children play with guns, needles, and human remains.

114

Last night, I plunged a portable fan into the sink and ploughed a travel adaptor into the shaving socket, and my body left behind a burning smell that made me cry.

115

New-regime nonexistence is an especially atrophied state of nonexistence.

116

False tranquility by any artificial swamp frees us momentarily from the blood sting, but if you're immune, the resistance is over.

117

The bodies hanging in the training hall dripped the blood of others, and the ropes, and the ropes, and the skin, and the skin, and the mess on the floor.

118

Those old-regime murder dreams of bloodstained bedsheets, of being hunted through shifting buildings and landscapes, used to scrape the gunk from our skullcaps, but in this post-regime haze, we are the nightmare.

119

After the end of civilization, we slumped down the steps into the lounge, and we sat staring at ourselves in a blank TV.

120

Satanic graphics in my notebook glow through slats in the hallway cupboard.

121

For sale: Generation Bloodbath T-shirt. Abused.

122

A: Keep a record of what happens, where, when, who, how.
T: The more details the better.
A: Ignore the veneer.
T: Words, ideas, thoughts, perceptions, feelings.
C: I'm unable to think straight.
A: This marks a development.
C: Why is a knife in the back of my neck?

123

There was a mechanical typewriter, two chairs, and a bed.

124

It was neither therapeutic nor traumatic, neither gift nor curse.

125

A knife to the neck is as good as a bullet to the brain for a dead child.

126

While writing these words on the back of your thigh,

between the veins, I discovered a scar, hiding there like the sail from a shipwreck washed into the desert and sunk there until someone dug it up and discovered a way to project our dreams upon its ghostly surface.

127

I climbed out of bed and limped to the blood-smeared window and watched the city burning.

128

New-regime nostalgia netted the greatest increase in patricides since statistics began.

129

I can cut, cut, cut because I've been working on my cutting hands, but if I never cut, cut, cut another, at least I've cut, cut, cut a real one.

130

We speak for the rats of the spaceships of the new worlds when we talk about blood.

131

I wander from the compound, through the light snow, to the river's edge, where I kneel and meditate over the suicide trains.

132

Downtown, bracketed from student anti-resistance protesters, I stutter into an old-regime diner, sipping my coffee and spinning my murder credentials (fifty prostitutes, eighty adults, ninety-two children), "And last time a major earthquake struck, I spent a decade in space!"

133

> G: Can't we talk this over?
> P: Death is my only friend.
> Z: What happened to my battle jacket?
> P: You need another cut.
> G: Don't touch me.
> Z: Is this a real ship?
> P: Try drinking the water.
> G: My blood is not to suck.
> P: Guess what's for lunch.
> Z: Breakfast?

134

As a gameshow, *Degenerate Stars* was aesthetically and conceptually derivative, but it achieved its aim of reducing the world's population by two thirds.

135

If you lie in a certain position and breathe in a certain rhythm, you might enter a dream where this bloodbath assassination simulation never happened (ketchup and corpse paint).

136

The trip of writing without the worry of being read is the closest we come to grace.

137

The graffiti under the train bridge probably meant the world to whoever wrote it, but I was too tired to open my eyes, let alone read.

138

A hammer in the face (88): I doubt us already.

139

The taste in our throats is the living things in the dead things in the living things in the dead things in the bloodbath backwash of new-regime clarity.

140

In old-regime linguistics, all language is a ghost haunted by other ghosts, or so says the sound coming from the head of a decapitated rat, somewhere in the dust and guts under the floorboards, where the carpet meets the wall, in our bedroom/spaceship.

141

The old-regime's unexpected comeback and its rebound in bloodshed is good news for speedboats.

142

Amputating the hands of infants symbolized new-regime superiority.

143

In neo-regime iconography, however, the only goal grander than killing the pregnant is impregnating the killed (zombie cannibal necrophilia).

144

Although the resistance origin story situates itself in a network of abandoned prisons, motels, and shopping malls, most splinter groups argue elsewhere.

145

We moved down the Blood Red River (cell membranes on motorcycles).

146

Terminal K came to an end.

147

When the resistance turned reactionary, the regime turned up the taps.

148

My face is a roadmap of crumbling lines, and my body is a stalled vehicle, but my blood continues to pump out along the highway.

149

I unfold the map, and/or the map unfolds me.

150

We huddle around the fire in the cave on the beach and tell each other stories about the way life never was and never will be (jet packs for suicide belts).

151

The elevator doors down the hallway open intermittently, closing six seconds later, and a green balloon hangs in the shaft.

152

The interrogation room pretends to have no exit (impostor syndrome).

153

The premise of *Backpackers Trashed by Axes* is six backpackers, one couple and two pairs of friends, arriving on an island promoting life-detox, physical and spiritual cleansing, and consciousness raising, so handing over your belongings is the price you pay the ferryman.

154

And as in any good movie, the cast gets killed at the end.

155

A: What are the rules of Generation Bloodbath?

T: There are no rules.

A: Are we there yet?

T: Yes.

C: But we haven't left.

156

On planets such as ours, where inhabitants are compliant, a speck of madness can distort results of sophisticated linguistic experiments conducted by demons/visitors.

157

Swimming in rivers of our own blood (speedboats on auto fuel), we chant resistance slogans until we drown, unless death comes first from blood loss (double win).

158

The resistance manifesto's opening pages call for absolute revolution.

159

Rotten bodies buried in the sand seek revenge for their violent sleep.

160

They had me pinned to a rail on an overpass, and they were about to dump me onto the traffic curving up from the city into a tunnel half-buried in clouds of yellow smoke drifting east.

161

Remember the Degenerate Star 666 Digital Deluxe Death Watch ($65.99 from all good retailers) and how wrist comforting it felt at first, and how it read your vital signs before morphing with the flesh to remove your limbs without amputation?

162

Let us forget.

163

The physiology of this world deals with the accumulation of blood.

164

One day it doesn't heal.

165

The old-regime answer to every question was "When all rivers run red."

166

Under the new regime, the leading cause of death became autoerotic asphyxiation culminating in spontaneous human combustion (speedboat to the stars).

167

The opening tracking shot of *Backpackers Attacked by Axes* lasts twenty-two hours without a cut before a backpacker is attacked by an axe.

168

During most mornings in the old-regime's early days, the clock on the nightstand was a wheelchair approaching a precipice, the overpass sign removed, and the carpet in the hallway reverted to a darker shade and texture, and the walls in the hallway ran with blood.

169

They grabbed my hair, dragged me down the hallway, smashed my face against the toilet bowl, then doused the house in gasoline before sharing a cigarette.

170

Tomorrow saw the sun die, a sacred chant to close every mantra.

171

Chunks of uncooperative corpse-waste flooded the desert surrounding the interrogation camp.

172

Attempting suicide after sleep, either by stabbing yourself or otherwise demolishing your body, is a golden flagstone path to freeze feelings of indifference in these dead lands.

173

Rumors of a way off the ship came coded as a trap, but some rats gobbled the space bait.

174

We make an educational pilgrimage detour to The Blood Licking Wall, where other freedom fighters used to face the firing squad, and we lick the wall, and the firing squad fires.

175

If you blame the visitors for infecting us with language, the old regime will remain where it remains in other regimes.

176

Remember the goons preaching a pre-regime dreamtime (they died no more or less a nightmare than us or them or anyone or those of us science set free from what we are or were genetically, grammatically, satanically, royalty-free)?

177

G: I suffer from travel sickness, narcolepsy, insomnia, apotemnophilia, kleptomania, schizophrenia, and countless unknown conditions.
P: You should learn to count.
G: (writing in fog on the porthole/portal) I was buried in the woods.
P: I wasn't expecting to help you die.
G: You were too wasted to move.

178

When the angelic visitors convinced us that they were locals, we left this planet as we found it, desolate and bloody.

179

Trapped in this ship, with this fragile orchestra of enforced delusions and the heart's faulty memories, brain tumors and aneurysms, my capacity to perform goal-directed actions independent of conscious volition disappears through the endless blood swill.

180

People become unusually calm when they've made an irreversible decision, and calmer after it's been acted upon, but between these syllables I'm gibbering, crying, sweating, laughing, freaking out at the gruesome details in my head.

181

Resistance journal writing advice: assassinate your eyeballs, firebomb your braincells.

182

I've had to deal with jerks and losers pretending to be me all my life, so I agree it's aggravating and potentially unsafe, but I don't consider it plagiarism or identity theft.

183

The illusion of a dead person with whatever backstory the impersonator wants to create remains an illusion.

184

I might have stabbed them to death and stuck my arm inside them, ventriloquist-style, to make it appear they were talking, but I've only ever been haunted by their beauty.

185

Gender and generation division were old-regime concepts introduced to sell subliminally infected breakfast cereal and other cloying works of cultural caricature.

186

We were programed to buy reality as a redemptive metaphor for our own lost youth, these broken sounds, words, and images a cruel link, an infinite torture porn of regret.

187

Our atoms are an identical interior version of our exterior actions, the swarming torment we enact in bloodbath fields, and in other outward states, such as degenerate stars collapsing.

188

And drugs and sex and violence and yoga (Extreme Youth).

189

Self-immolation + levitation: the only way to fly (speedboat to the stars).

190

The new regime proved itself more satanic than the old regime, which had defined itself as the only god by being so brutal we forgot all previous narratives of control.

191

Leaflets in phone boxes, somehow the only objects left standing in the city, called for random strangers to research which body parts were responsible for murdering other body parts.

192

When the resistance paused resisting, the neo regime devolved into a parody of old-regime brutality.

193

They taught us the physics of asphyxiation, the chemistry of immolation, and the biology of seppuku.

194

Post-regime proverb: the claw digging into your head might have belonged to you previously, but the force comes from elsewhere and so does the head.

195

I crawl from the cave onto a deserted beach.

196

I gaze into the blood box containing my fallen teeth.

197

The only resistance flag is a battle jacket on fire.

198

Somehow, we survived.

199

A: Look through the telescope.

T: Which direction?

A: Not over there.

T: I've gone blind.

A: To the left.

T: What is it?

A: Probably another ghost ship.

T: Why are they doing this to us?

A: Don't take it personally.

200

The neo regime occupies a narcotic brain high on language.

201

It's impossible to disappear if we were never here, but blood speaks louder than epistemology, and a knife in the face speaks louder than a stamp on the passport.

202

The end of grammar was the end of time.

203

Murder went to my chest, and I failed to wash the blood from under my floorboards.

204

The original tables in the night market were not constructed from bones but from firebombed forests in the new-regime's early days when the resistance was unborn.

205

The new-regime compound in the desert is larger than the new world.

206

I follow the tape marking the compound's parameters and listen to bicycles shadowing me, because they've been told I believe in escape and freedom, and my eyes are a blood swamp.

207

The sight of a child's blue bicycle, buckled and rusted, abandoned in a highway ditch, is more powerful and profound than the mountain of decapitation in the city of long nights.

208

Then came another end, and it was not the end.

209

If they wanted us dead, we'd be dead.

210

A: (Clear light) What's the matter with you?

T: (Tear gas) You didn't answer my question.

C: (Gagging on each other's love) We swallowed too many pills, went for a walk in the rain.

T: (Clear light) What were we unclothing?

A: (Tear gas) I identified the body. Someone took an earring.

211

In the field behind the barn, a wall of amplifiers emits a subsonic drone.

212

The world's highest number of mountain-six assassination attempts in one day contaminated my memory and all I do now is wake up drink coffee go to work go home get drunk watch TV go to sleep wake up drink coffee go to work go home get drunk watch TV go to sleep.

213

Our conversation continued with a predictable new-regime critique, so I left the tent, and I climbed over the rocks, and I sat down and listened to the bombs pounding the city.

214

Crows swoop in front of freight trains overloaded with those feasting on the dead.

215

Experimenting with phantom-limb torture and re-amputation procedures, the neo regime re-chopped the children of the night market.

216

They named us Young Rats (Extreme Youth) initially because of our inclination to gnaw ourselves and each other to death.

217

The resistance calls the moment before the axe strikes the back of your neck "the purest and most beautiful form of devotion and subjectivity."

218

We took a shower together, and we got into bed, and some time passed where nothing happened, and I thought this was going nowhere, so I repeated some random lies.

219

For the revolution: love songs, grand imitation narratives, open doorways, tailbone bathtubs, boiling cattle, a moth hovering around a lamp, a wig sticking out from under a bush, and a strap going through a buckle in clear Technicolor light.

220

The TV-FUZZ Award for Greatest Atrocity went to someone who worked at the network.

221

Most nights in the dining hall, the captain eats and drinks the flesh and blood of us below the deck, but the scene gets spine-chilling when he calls for the wine.

222

On butcher paper, the voice of negation writes in blood: yes.

PART 333

Into the Void

Rocket engines burning fuel so fast
Up into the night sky they blast

223

After I miss my boarding call and make an offhand comment about temporality, I get upgraded to first class, and after thirty minutes, someone threatens to blow up the plane, and after sixty minutes, someone blows up the plane, and it breaks apart and comes back.

224

Heads explode on TVs in motel rooms.

225

Enter the Arena (bloodbath extracurricular archive warehouse): the crowd goes wild, and more bodies explode (relief from torture endured).

226

The party was over before the party started, and we were vomiting blood, but love is a rope, and our necks love to swing.

227

Sabotage the cocktail bars and erect the insurrection!

228

The new regime wheels out rusty contraptions to print simulation sweatshop T-shirts with deliberately misspelled characters representing its manifesto.

229

With the rope around my neck, I feel resistance glory, and the more I struggle, the more the regimes goad me to disgust.

230

This corpse's surface, collapsing between us, slowly at the edge, is a foolish mistake, a reckless career move, unlike my love of housebreaking and goon-stalking.

231

The night-market rats learned to transcend their blood tanks (all hail the golden bullets).

232

Temples burned marijuana to cover the smell of the living eating the dead.

233

A: How was your violent sleep?
T: Where are we?
A: Talking sense is dangerous.
C: I want to go back.
A: Say some different words.
T: I can't move.
C: I've gone blind.
T: Let's locate some more drugs.
A: This place is dosed and loaded.

234

We were the visitors, and they were here first (jet packs for suicide belts).

235

Vivisection unearthed weapons (such as guns, knives, and explosives) buried deep in the children of the night market.

236

Ritually cooking children in vegetable oil, after draining their blood, is more nursery rhyme than mercy crime, because their fluid brings little cash to fuel the speedboats.

237

Another occupational anomaly is brainwashing the brainwashed, although reeducating splinter-cult defectors might be more of a calling than a dirt-cheap deed done dirty.

238

They drove the resistance so far underground it appeared forever internal lava would imprint the new-regime insignia into our golden bullets.

239

Our sickness remembers, probably a panic invasion, or a calculated attack, but before the old regime, and after the new regime, dynamically between paradoxes, they called us gone, bewitched by the shape of our own hands, playing with dead rats, buried rats, alone.

240

It's obscenely easy to lure trust-fund backpackers to a cabin on an island, particularly when they believe it's a reality show, and—after a drink or two, or six—into a bathtub of blistering crystals and healing kerosene.

241

I discovered an infant on the highway halting the mourning parade of no cars passing.

242

After the final funeral, we inhaled heavy metal from air conditioners, hands growing sideways, bodies curled up on the floor, derailing the narrative drive.

243

On the top floor of an abandoned skyscraper, a wall of amplifiers emits a subsonic drone.

244

Z: Let me feel how your hands feel.

P: Those are empty words.

Z: The light on your ears as the clouds vanish, the breeze when we get each other off, rubbing barbwire between our legs.

P: You're not listening.

Z: I dare you to jump.

P: Sure. Go first.

245

The regime taught us a private language after we underwent surgery leaving us inarticulate and incoherent.

246

I might be ecstatic and filled with revelations I want to share with the world, or I might be in shock, repeating one word from the whatever many hundred were left after the virus gobbled our language, but my head is a circuit board no soldering can fix.

247

Kidnapping and decapitating landlords became necessary to obtain shelter.

248

Dear diary, today I give up.

249

Regime beach towns never attracted tourists but cults and spiritualists and ghost hunters and goons and gurus and drug fiends and rapists, and the sand and the water were red.

250

A bloody gunk patch spread, contracted, and dangled from the ceiling in a glistening drop.

251

Outside on the balcony, in the humidity, I glance down at cicadas littering the road, fireworks littering the alley, and dead children oozing in the rice fields.

252

Particularly when penetration and ejaculation culminated in inventive acts of homicide, old-regime reverse psychology encouraged all forms of sexual abuse.

253

If the resistance goes to sleep, it will wake up more resistant (ketchup and corpse paint).

254

Riverbank: melted photographs of meat wrapped in plastic and tied up with string in a soggy cardboard box, a cattle truck, a disused chimney, and here comes another false memory of a swimming pool, shadow lines on a rooftop dissecting a suntanned torso.

255

With our spines broken, we hope for a quick death, or at least one that hammers quickly.

256

Structure exceeded = automatic sadism + automatic masochism, and there is no context.

257

Smell is the second last sensation left in our impotent

speedboat loop.

258

The loudest sounds are the scratching of pens on paper and the beating of limbs on sand.

259

For revolution to happen, there must be space, space, space; otherwise, the world freezes.

260

To die by LSD and angel dust is to join the never dead.

261

I find myself brain-damaged and barely conscious three months later.

262

Night markets selling new-regime souvenirs resurface on reclaimed blood swamps, and reticently the resistance bombs fall.

263

For each new-regime Atrocity, the neo regime commits a million.

264

Existence was only a virus for those who expired before us, or before our eyes, ears, noses, mouths, hands were tortured senseless.

265

Vanishing Act (33): old-regime comically colossal instrument of gore, becomes new-regime spontaneous heart attack, becomes neo-regime unsighted disappearance (i.e., evaporation phobia), but as soon as the body returns, we're back in the muck.

266

A: What do you want to talk about?

T: The phone boxes.

A: Happy or sad?

T: Off the scale.

A: I can smell the bodies under the floorboards.

T: Is there a drug to dehydrate them?

A: Peppermint oil and boiling water.

T: Love is complicated.

267

Crows swoop in front of suicide trains and live to tell, but when deleted people try to fly the same way, they get their headphones or shoelaces tangled, mangled, crushed, dead, dust.

268

The regime remained in power longer than power remained.

269

Self-murder was the only option for those unable to accept the satanic trinity of signs.

270

On the road out of town, we pass a caravan identical to the one with which we are riding, except for one crucial difference: the drivers are headless, and the passengers are gone.

271

Knowledge was a thing.

272

We smell like kenneled dogs waiting for the incinerator.

273

Under a bathtub, abandoned in a cave along the coast, sits a Blood Cube replica with more power than the original, and the blanket covering the replica says more blood must flow.

274

The regime removed the maps (negative forecasting) before the ships departed.

275

In a split universe, the ships shatter, and my head is filled with cold water, burning buildings, plagiarized memories, imprisonment and sex slavery, and the chunks on my knife are the days of my life, all tasting the opposite of love.

276

The neo regime claimed it represented a blank slate beyond languages and genetic programs, those lineage constraints, but their reality is a fractured internal interview with a busted mouth, running its tongue around gums missing teeth and lips pouring blood lines.

277

In new-regime propaganda mythology, the resistance splinters into esoteric religious groups taking up arms against each other in a holy war.

278

I snatched at the silver barrel of a Walther P22, pressing against my chest, and braced myself for the entrance wound.

279

Two backpackers scuttled over the walls, and got lost in a swamp, and they are currently being attacked by invisible and extremely rare bugs.

280

I follow a goon gang inside the house, and we play rogue shadow-puppet states on the walls, but I can't sleep, so I count a hundred degenerate stars outlining a proxy regime of regrets.

281

Exhausted from resisting the battle internal, we resigned ourselves to haunting the new regime through telepathic signals on cereal boxes.

282

The old-regime axiom translates to "The blood we shed makes our own blood purer," but the new regime added a clause about "blackening our hearts."

283

Time slowed down so much we stopped calling it time.

284

It starts with a nosebleed, bathroom mirror reflection, and it ends with the end of the world.

285

I wake up drunk on the morning after the mourning parade.

286

Matchsticks hold my lids open as I scrape wax from my eyes with a box cutter, peel off layers of gunk, and curate a matchbox exhibition of Picnic of Six waxwork figures.

287

False confession (11): I have lived in the sun, and I have lived under a speedboat, and I have written journal entries about faces appearing on motel walls, infinite overdoses, rapes, tortures, break and enters, and mass murders, but I know nothing about the resistance.

288

A: What's written in your journal?

T: A superior replica, better than a duplicate.

A: Immortality is too much.

T: We're not what we thought we were.

A: Have you ever had lunch in a grindhouse cinema?

T: Torture porn keeps me cold.

289

Life became a limited series of untangling knives from kitchen draws, and the stab and the stabbing, and the slash and the slashing, and the brutal charade of defense wounds.

290

Neo-regime entertainment included administering TX4 hypodermics to induce hypnotic heart attacks in anyone who ever considered revolution.

291

Post-regime death-cult goons roamed the gloomy, war-torn streets in shabby animal suits.

292

I'm writing this down to make sure, after it's happened and I'm filming myself, I've got a script to follow, although I'm not sure how strictly I'll be able to stick to the script, or in what state of unison my voice and body parts will be operating.

293

Resistance songs are the same, lyrically, as their regime counterparts, but articulation differs when the vocal apparatus has been cut.

294

Drinking blood might keep us alive, but the life we live should be renamed bleeding.

295

Whenever airplanes explode in reverse, I think of you (pyrotechnics).

296

Generation Bloodbath drifts above whatever naive narrative pins us to the naming maze.

297

I have a nightmare.

298

Conveniently "abandoned" in a demolished apartment, a suicide backpack, stuffed with poorly forged old-regime banknotes, is an enduring and distressing revolution symbol.

299

Jerking Off in the Devil's Face (JODF) was a hokey, pseudo-regime, summer-camp magazine, initiation campaign designed to signify the ultimate satanic rejection of antiquated human concepts such as the bad, the evil, the other, the wrong.

300

And the words were back on my lips, breaking the lengthy, dead silence between us, as I climbed on a ledge with a burnt stick resembling a prehistoric axe handle.

301

The original axes trashing the backpackers in *Backpackers Trashed by Axes* hang behind flameproof glass in the New Regime Film Academy's (NRFA) Hall of Fame.

302

This corpse paint ain't cursed to rot.

303

Smoke from coastal cannibal factories forms predictably ominous patterns in the yellow sky above the Bloodbath Sea (fog machines).

304

My brain was wired and defined by the regime as an alleyway where suicides, overdoses, car jobs, and other victims of murder or misadventure huddle behind a washed-out strip club.

305

Written by numbers, new-regime algorithms in our extracellular DNA waged war with themselves, a radical autoimmunity.

306

When the satanic visitors convinced us that they were locals, we left this planet as we found it, devoted and beautiful.

307

The resistance meant more to us than the regimes we were resisting.

308

Ten grams in deathtrip neon (if you want to kill someone, don't research how to do it, don't bleed out the window, and don't talk through languages anyone comprehends).

309

The butterfly is a freak for the new regime.

310

P: What generation are you?
G: Generation-666.
P: Ah, I knew it. Show me something.
G: Like what?
P: Like anything.
G: We're not human. We're metal.
Z: We think ... Or so we think.

311

I write hysterical poems about visitor abduction because this house sits on stilts, and it moves as a boat lost at sea, and some goons in white suits have poured gasoline on my back, and they're about to set me on fire with a lighted candle handed to them by a tarot-card reader.

312

Existence differing from official truth is strangled and led away in handcuffs, but autopsy stamps give the official cause of death as injury by a single bullet to the head.

313

The post-regime answer to every question was "When the bloodbath resumes."

314

Sleeping in a beach crevice, which has been old-regime

gutted, I witness this map become a passage, split worlds in bones abandoned, and in this ship's hull, elaborate nothingness transforms abstract power into a lurid ghost teacher guiding the axe in my hand.

315

If the days felt protracted during the new regime, it's because they were.

316

Twenty-five percent of the three billion prisoners shot by the old regime were posthumously recruited into the new regime.

317

Psychogenic oral paresthesia paved the way for post-regime paranoia.

318

Glitches in the metaphor (27): a juvenile sucking on a revolver says, "The resistance is for the adults never loving us and the tears never drying."

319

They were dead on the lawn outside the house next door.

320

In this infinite, teensploitation, procedurally generated wilderness, we walk in bloodbaths of our own blood with our brains razor spliced in half (ketchup and corpse paint), because who can say what the end brings, and who cares, anyway, if we're high (speedboat to the stars).

321

A: You want it bloodier?
T: They can't touch us.

A: I heard otherwise.

T: Is a gun to the head worse than two to the guts?

A: I foresee much spillage.

T: In the new regime, nothing can't be mangled.

A: With a face to crush the resistance, I feel unsealed.

T: Yours ashore.

A: Never live through this...

322

Language sets us free.

323

Another life, another homage, enough blood, enough.

324

Existence is no excuse through new-regime eyes.

325

Severin Island, where they filmed *Backpackers Trashed by Axes*, was a former virus colony littered with skeletons rising from the grave to trash the cast and crew with ornamental axes brought as props (cinéma vérité).

326

If animal amputation carries any weight, the children of the night market are less idiotic than their elders, but the books they read arc a hcarsc.

327

Hundreds of amputated infants hang naked from the rafters in each neo-regime community center throughout the colonies, and still the ropes hang still.

328

In a neo-regime archive warehouse, painstakingly arranged

piles of glass spin phantom mirror dreams: three rolls of masking tape, two blowtorches, a handful of lollipops and other candies, a bucketful of cocaine, the old-world currency of pain and desire.

329

The bloodbaths return night after night, which makes sense if we consider what other voices were heard here and there before the neo-regime's revolutionary guards got hip.

330

At a truck stop near The Blood Licking Wall, we step over potholes of blood (the staff had been tortured with coat hangers for thirty-three days, or so we were told by the tour guide).

331

Blood for the sake of blood is the best sort of blood.

332

When the blood runs dry, we run through that old trick with the wine.

333

In the absence of absinthe, we face the firing squad.

PART 444

Snowblind

What you get and what you see

Things that don't come easily

334

Generation Bloodbath was spray-painted on the side of a white van belonging to a heavy metal band.

335

They came through the stairs and the walls and the flames attacking us.

336

They dragged us to the lounge room and sat us on the carpet near the entertainment system and played us the latest Atrocity videos and shot us in the heads.

337

The donkey-child of the new regime was king.

338

Various tactical displacement formulas (shadow-puppet-state tetraphobia) led me to the fourth level of a building, where miniature rooms without doors went nowhere until the beginning from the end.

339

The Regime Knows (season three, episode five): insane reading of unwritten monologue lost in this blood swill we thought we awoke from with the new regime gone.

340

Millions of infants were soaked in gasoline and burned and raped, but their smiles were inflamed with abrupt feelings of freedom (neo-regime advertising campaign).

341

The relics unearthed in the desert were fake, but the bloodbath they unleashed was real.

342

And the blood for sale was not the blood we sold (counter switch to fuel the speedboats).

343

A cocaine shipment washes up on a deserted beach on Severin Island.

344

A: I dreamed about people jumping off buildings.

T: I want to commit suicide, but I don't want to die.

A: I saw a leg twitching, a body convulsing.

C: Lizards in the desert bleed from their eyes.

A: I want to see your eyes bleed.

T: I thought you'd say that.

A: I know.

345

Torture porn formed the world from outer space, a collection of atoms.

346

They call us frantically romantic creatures, and we call them psychotically satanic leeches.

347

Resistance mantra (1,914): keep the shades open, so they can assess your existence.

348

The brake was released on the collision-dowse button, and, landing in acid vats, the teenagers shouted specific subliminal slogans signifying their undying commitment to the revolution.

349

Strangulation robots removed the carpet from the hallway.

350

Under broken floorboards, broken bodies float in saltwater, corpse paint cooked by the sun.

351

If not for the blood on our hands, all the bodies messed up squirming under the floorboards might let us sleep.

352

Willful ignorance is a byproduct of brain mechanics, over which people cannot be expected to exercise control, so our moral and legal judgments rest on bloody ground.

353

There are carp swimming in a blood stream flowing through a mass-grave expressway, over vegetable markets and glass elevators, and the taxi slows down as the traffic builds up, and this is a time when nothing matters outside exiting the city.

354

I pull a spent shell from my pocket and hand it over as a peace offering, an act of devotion, initiation, or intimidation (who knows?), but never for what I've done.

355

P: If someone wrote a book about your life, what would they call it?

G: I've never been truly drunk.

P: You shouldn't think so much.

Z: I need a new blender to get drunk.

G: I saw a blender, years ago, a tranquil light burning in time.

P: What about everyone else?

356

In a crater in the desert, a wall of amplifiers emits a subsonic drone.

357

Dig the vampires (incoming teeth-torture manifesto)!

358

The symptoms of vampire attacks bring us ecstasy, but our language has been reduced to two words articulated through infinite inflections of deference to the neo regime.

359

Pre-regime memory (18): a veterinary student hacks out my tonsils with a dirty knife, and the infection fills my vocal apparatus with pop-song-lyric obscenity.

360

Confused veterinary lecturers wheeled me, singing in a state of bovinity, around corridors, displaying me to students, and grading the angles in which they sliced my mouth.

361

I was taken to a doctor, who prodded my stomach and told the vets to take me to a hospital, where I was cut open, and some miniature weapons were removed, and the weapons were arranged in a snow globe, pieces floating in liquid through sunshine on a dashboard.

362

On the horizon is the regime's golden column, in the mirror is an overflowing bloodbath.

363

A simulated sun sets over the Bloodbath Sea.

364

And in the end, the bloodbath you take is equal to the bloodbath you make.

365

The refugee complex surrounds the grave complex, headlights drifting around the streets, people marching slowly toward death over volcanic rocks in the moonlight, freezing and dehydrated, chest pain, panic attacks, altitude sickness in cramped suburban hell.

366

Millions marched to the mountains with holes in their heads and danced with cows in the fields and died in the sunshine (rotting, soil, grass, flowers).

367

The virus demolished our more crystalline concepts and left us trampling through this voiceless gunk, seeking a darker exit.

368

From a rope in a new-regime training hall, I gaze down, head lopsided, wondering if anyone realizes how good this feels, how challenging it is to hold on, and how much I want to let go despite being broken.

369

Neo-regime proverb: just because a limb is healthy does not mean the leg is real.

370

Blood addiction (contact, taste, rush, overdose, detox) produces more junkies than other junk.

371

We spoke together to forget the forest where we died.

372

Skin hangs flopped from wooden pegs, blood dripping, and we sober up in the morning, mumbling alcohol passion, under the hammer, the wrench, the crowbar, the clamp, garbage caught under our hooves, in a barnyard quarter in a karaoke town.

373

Four months later, I'll be found dead in a different shopping mall.

374

The civilization who lived in peace, as a spiritual action, and the soldiers who decapitated babies, as a political action, all die in the same pot of boiling plasma to fuel the spaceships.

375

Furnaces in the southern refineries breathed as our husks burned yellow and our nightmares returned to smoke (fog machines at dawn).

376

They would have used chemical or nuclear weapons if they hadn't wanted to use our blood to fuel the spaceships.

377

A: I don't want to cut you anymore.
T: Why did you bring me here?

A: Never ask a question if you possess the answer.

T: How long have you been cutting me?

A: For money?

T: For cutting.

A: Think of this as a death trip.

T: I'm pretty much a failure in life.

A: What day is it?

378

Those who promoted Virtual Mutiny Visualization (VMV), to remove our astral bodies from our physical ones, never studied the horrors of escape-time mining in a hole, in a box, underground.

379

Blood Yoga levitation brings the mountains to us, and brings us to the mountains, but the speedboats suck us to the stars.

380

If the resistance was a tattoo on your arm, the ink would fade with the blood you shed.

381

The new-regime's cheapest trick was pretending it was post regime (ketchup and corpse paint).

382

The taste in my mouth is the taste of my mouth.

383

You awoke after three days, sat up, and stretched your arms.

384

The movement of blood encased within the internal walls left feathering patterns and light shadows like a collection of tortoise shells and discarded fishing line.

385

In the squalor, we live, and in the squalor, we die, and each moment between is an effort to jam the meat grinder scattering those who came before us.

386

The decomposed bodies found under the house had been stored in boxes lined with aluminum foil, but there were no other indications of space travel.

387

All hail the golden bullets in a hail of bullets across the yellow sky on the new-sky planet.

388

The taxi driver knows my name, but I don't, and we swerve around the tanks.

389

Feelings work through interpretive thought systems, but broken pieces of flesh, silence, noise, and vibration suggest nothing is everything (onward we go nowhere).

390

I'm conscious enough to glean some emotions from them, but their skin's been crudely swabbed in blue paint, wounds stitched up with brown string, mouths wrapped shut with coat hangers, and eyes blasted out with a nail gun, but they continue to stare at the shattered TV.

391

The old regime calls our language a virus, and the new regime calls our body a virus, and the resistance calls the words we hear untrue.

392

Karmic Verdict (39): the surgery, the courtroom, the morgue (and vice versa).

393

Congratulations, I'll kill us both (all).

394

The medicalization of capital punishment radically expanded poetry's role in human consciousness, but the lethal injection was inferior to a junky's delicate ritual.

395

After injecting expired morphine and drinking old-regime coffee, instead of blood-soaked wine, I experienced a clarity better than viewing a body as simply this sketchily named collection of constituent parts containing other constituent parts.

396

The *Backpackers Attacked by Axes* TV series is as good as or better than the original film.

397

New regime logic: children with no arms, heaving shopping carts along rubble highways, only dream of maps and signs and broken teeth.

398

For those of us left resisting, dragnet corpses caught in unending tunnels under new-regime sewers became a charcoal feast.

399

    P: Generation Bloodbath will set us free.

    G: Freedom is the price we pay.

    Z: Our blood is not your blood.

    P: Your freedom is not your freedom.

    G: Blood is the only commodity.

    Z: Our price is not your price.

    P: Stay with the resistance.

    G: Our resistance is your regime.

400

Hacking limbs off children, a most nostalgic post-regime mode of foreplay, cues the music warning nightfall.

401

Dusk seeps through palm trees at the end of the final funeral day, and headless corpses on the beach enact a peculiar masochistic achievement of posthumous self-pregnancy, but there is nothing better in the world than watching the sunset on security monitors.

402

Yellow clouds filled the city as the night bus pulled onto the demolished highway.

403

Blood stained the road, and the road stained the blood.

404

Speech became a head wound, written words a blood clot (period).

405

The new-regime answer to every question was "When the waste land is a blood bath."

406

The resistance manifesto's last page calls for an end to manifestos.

407

We, the resistance revolutionaries, reject with a decapitated NO, any regime in which the visitors behave as free particles consuming human flesh.

408

Next new-regime strategy: all bombs explode before lunch (pyrotechnics).

409

Leaving for the Ministry of Unknown Affairs (MUA), I notice blood-soaked clothing exhumed from the garbage, and I look back at my apartment to see the curtains catch fire.

410

I shelter in a telephone box.

411

I squeeze through the space between stairways, and I climb over barbwire fences, and the feeling in my guts is a lyric death poem, an undefined apocalyptic farce.

412

For each Atrocity committed in the name of the pseudo regime, those recorded in the Snuff Corpus, a million went unnoticed, and the infinite other possibilities unperformed carried enough weight to tilt a black hole off its axis.

413

Microwave ovens explode in suburban homes.

414

Recent arrivals to the colony bring other viruses, other ways to bleed our consciousness.

415

When people disappear here, their shells continue cruising for blood.

416

Old-regime proverb: the claw digging into your head might belong to you for now, but the force comes from elsewhere and so does the hand.

417

The perfect film shows blood and semen on the walls of a prison cell (motel room).

418

The playback experience paradox of pseudo-regime quantum mechanics is crushed and heavy, but it remains a cruel wedge, draining humanity in rebirth-recurrence bloodshed.

419

Comprehending what's happened is impossible, and I'm tired of philosophy, and afraid of unrequited love, fatal injuries soaked in clockwork, gushing letter psychology, and detective methodology, but the cream the visitors apply is cool, and it makes the bite marks fade.

420

The telephone on the table rings if you stare at it and contemplate it ringing, but there's no one in the room to pick it up, and the bodies in the hallway have no limbs.

421

A: (I need oxygen) Don't you enjoy any movies?

T: (I crave a subplot) Commercials are all I can stand.

C: (I could explode) What are you talking about?

T: (Imagine the laughter) Did you ask me what I was doing?

A: (I was delusional) I found your number in my pocket.

422

To die in this world, whatever the drug, is the least of our worries.

423

In the flickering TV light, I smoked and watched you sleeping.

424

Without regret, there'd be nothing left.

425

Unconscious language constituted the reference point, denied and restored in the external wounds of identity crisis, which continued going down to rot and soak in hydrochloric acid methamphetamine, making objective alienation an admirable quality.

426

We were removed from consideration, excluded from survival, but nothing differs in space.

427

Had we not discovered the enjoyment of eating our own, we would have surrendered much more blood to the new regime.

428

The way we move within the wires, avoiding the wires (and

the blood and the blood etc.) before falling dead bloodless (fuel the speedboats), makes music many find appalling, but others worship, and others pay to experience, because wherever there's a blood show...

429

The most depressing characteristic of the neo-regime's nostalgic retro mania is the infinite recycling and rearranging of a finite number of cliches.

430

DNA examination confirmed original cave art, created by spray cans of blood paint, depicting a million massacres.

431

Backpackers Trashed by Axes: names and circumstances have been changed for dramatic purposes, and out of respect for the victims and their families, but all dialogue is real.

432

Z: You want it bloodier? I demand ritual DECAPITATION.
P: The storage facilities on this ship are generally inadequate.
Z: Toss my HEAD to the waves.
P: Embalming of fatal injuries is praised.

433

The new regime launched a counter campaign painting themselves as victims of a deliberately insane reading of history (jet packs for suicide belts).

434

Witnessing your family members being shot in the head is no joke, but plugging their wounds with mud and straw is a valid pastime.

435

Infomercial: I recommend Blood Placebo because the price is never cooked in junk-mail combustibles.

436

The bile in my mouth, from where the new regime grabbed, twisted, and removed my internal organs, and ritually set them on fire, although it cannot be proven, is partly responsible for me maintaining this singsong slang, this private-detective dialect.

437

Discharge stained the walls, breeding a new kind of mold, one which after ingestion induced false visions of a darker exit.

438

When we returned to the Blood Red River, the river was dry, and the banks were cracked, and the riverbed was closer to black.

439

"Make it bleed," we chant as one.

440

A stranger spy tells the landmine sky: "We slept here, obedient to our wounds, but a needle never came as close to the locus of pain as a knife did to the abdomen!"

441

The donkey who breaks the child's uterus (and/or *sphincter ani internus*)—expanding, ugly, the alphabet swollen into blobs of textual shock, the external organs a cocktail of sunburnt pink, a faded jingle from an ice cream van—is the donkey who runs the new regime.

442

It starts with a phone call, and it ends with the end of the world.

443

No magical narrative comforter could ward off the horror we felt at being set free.

444

Here come the vampires!

PART 555

Sabbath Bloody Sabbath

You've seen life through distorted eyes
You know you had to learn

445

At the start of twenty-five years' incarceration (torture for heretical poems, execution for political incest), I bite through the banister staring down at my own bloodbath.

446

The Antihuman Slaughter Agitation Group (ASAG) confused conservation with eradication, and this glitch resulted in annihilation never witnessed before.

447

We feel black rain coming in from the ocean, crows punching holes in the sand, crows hammering the bay, but in the morning, the palm trees have been touched up, and then a bulldozer crushes them, this set being recycled, and us being blood and bone and sand.

448

Dashboard cracks, foam burnt by the sun, remind me of cigarette marks made on your face, a hack-death-slasher final girl in a video store, marks becoming holes with a ballpoint pen, your body pretty much gone, ripped up like a magazine page by rogue-regime goons.

449

If it takes a bloodbath, let's take a drink.

450

The most beautiful sensations I remember are the abrupt feelings of potential freedom, the frantic voices whispering, withholding cartoon hysterics, and being excessively drunk.

451

My tooth floating in a wine glass is the final metaphor.

452

One night in a club, I was drinking with a gang of ex-regime goons, who said they were "asphyxiating on the atmosphere of existence," so I spilled for them my blood.

453

In an empty suburban swimming pool, a wall of amplifiers emits a subsonic drone.

454

The end of the world is the beginning of Generation Bloodbath.

455

G: Have you got a skateboard?

P: I had one somewhere... I can't remember.

Z: If you could have three superpowers, what would they be?

P: There's this hot adult human, but not as hot as a visitor.

G: Guess what's for lunch.

Z: Breakfast?

456

Choking to death on your own blood (heredity): a voyage beyond the stars.

457

We're so skinny, deflated balloons, the noose can't kill us.

458

The hand that signed the suicide note might have been mine, but it was no longer attached.

459

After sleep paralysis succeeds, the room becomes one with the eyelids, and the smell is a kind of robbery, morphine intoxicating, corpse distilling, the dissecting knife is covered with blood from the floor, and the hair is humidity-itchy and hacked off hot.

460

Stains on my burial T-shirt and battle jacket remind me of passing through the burning barn.

461

And what we saw this morning left many of us alive speechless and others unable or unwilling to prove themselves otherwise.

462

I hunch over in a lunchtime bar and watch my chewed fingernails grow in nanometers until I can employ them to scratch off enough wallpaper to construct a notebook.

463

I want to write you a poem combining violent sleep's insanely lesser conclusions with a body on the waves in the distance, a leaf in a swimming pool, and a bug swirling down the drain.

464

When the bomb hit, the archiving machinery collapsed, killing the people in the basement, and no one bothered sending in the dogs.

465

At the night market, blood comes with a plastic straw, and we rejoice the slaughter.

466

A: I don't know what they're talking about.
T: They don't know what they're talking about.
C: They might not be talking.

T: I'm going back to your videos.

A: Beauty and the surface are cheap language limitations.

T: What's the least traceable method?

A: No literature requires an author.

467

New-regime passport photo: a shotgun blast to the head.

468

Oxygen is overrated, and these tanks expired decades ago, but the rust exposure haunts us.

469

A radio in a motel room reports mass murder between the commercials.

470

Having been suspended from medical practice, I was running an underground clinic, where I systematically misdiagnosed the conditions of goons (not just a bit; not just in the way all medical people do. It encapsulated my entire corpus).

471

As our language functions collapsed, the scramble for an Alternative Communication System (ACS) became more absurd than the worst sci-fi conspiracy-theory satire.

472

It's fruitless printing hollow books, grungy bloodwork journals, and junky cannibal poems, to fling someone a furtive mess.

473

When one language remained, the last linguistic turn came as an autoimmune response infecting the virus and garbling the world.

474

The blood kept us indoors until the blood came indoors.

475

Hearts in the Acid River float above other organs, shrivel more slowly, continue to beat.

476

The stories they told us about the old planet were an attempt to plug us into gods greater than the gods of the new regime.

477

I walk around an apartment, clogged with deflated balloons, and I pass out on the couch.

478

We were afterbirth, rat-poison paraphernalia, paraded through subtropical prostitute districts, buried up to our armpits in pits of moist overdose.

479

The sound of flames turned into the sound of wings.

480

Birdsong in fall brought us closer to death, or what they used to call death.

481

After the real bloodbath, came the fake bloodbath (ketchup and corpse paint).

482

Footsteps and heartbeats synchronized, we're trudging

around a bombed expressway, circling the city, and this is the clockwork world the old regime promised to destroy.

483

Neo-regime radio update (356): the drug of choice for frontline fighters on the extragalactic front is an unknown agent mixed with the dust of shattered bones (degenerate stars).

484

The trick they taught us was not a trick; it was a way we thought they wanted us to think about the way they represented whatever they called thinking: the blood-splattered walls, the animal-death smell absent from horror films, an endless, almighty, space-time medicinal fix.

485

Our love for the resistance blossomed through language inscribed by the old regime on the cauterized organs we used to articulate this love.

486

The structural integrity of *Backpackers Trashed by Axes* is based on socially driven death occurring at the core of an inaccessible and unreceptive audience.

487

If you burn alive tonight at the point in your dreams where you connect with the ones who do for you whatever gets you through, you better burn baby burn, as the saying goes, or I'm coming for you, and your ashes are blood.

488

A: Why didn't you answer the phone?
P: I told you not to call the landline.

A: I never knew we were allowed shore leave.

P: You called five times last night.

A: I was drunk.

P: You need help.

A: You're the one who needs help.

P: Everyone was drunk.

A: I don't remember calling you.

P: That's why I didn't answer.

489

Being undercover became the only way of being (counter agent click track).

490

The day turned to napalm, and the neighbors turned to ash.

491

New-regime internship: I stood there all summer wearing headphones and injecting juveniles with cyanide.

492

I wish I was hallucinating those faces peering through the brickwork, white powdery blobs with matted hair and angry expressions, trying to mouth a warning I can't make out because the picture isn't dubbed and the subtitles have slipped off the screen, but this is real.

493

The world we lost wasn't the one we left, and the memories we predict won't become void, but those auto-fuel speedboats drain too much blood from our necks.

494

I forge a menu from chronic memory poems in a restaurant on the other side of town and order two child-steaks with identical-twin traumas.

495

The ghostwriters of our suicide notes, which contain several deliberate inaccuracies (coded resistance messages), went on to share the inaugural New Regime Award for Literature.

496

The word for Atrocity was lost in the velocity.

497

After grammar, I remember the end.

498

It was probably intentional on several levels, but I never deviate from the surface.

499

At least the adverts improved under the neo regime, and we could sky our hopes to the stake-grim reality of impossible rebirth shattered inside.

500

Stabbing someone ten million times isn't going to make them deader or less alive.

501

The radio: white leather case with stitches on the side, a cream speaker, two silver knobs, the left knob for power and volume, a buildup of pressure and then click, the other for tuning, a buffer at the end signaling time to turn back and explore elsewhere.

502

The trauma explored in the first remake of *Backpackers*

Attacked by Axes was made more dramatic by mechanisms often or usually associated with chopping.

503

My autopsy journal is completely fabricated, but my grip on the pen, and the shadow on the page, contain all the love left on Earth.

504

At night the blood blisters burst the bedsheets.

505

Flashback (45), traveling through alcoholic psychiatry: I'm standing beside my family in the kitchen of a disconnected display home, and the future is a non-unitary quantum gate.

506

The cane-machete ratio on Severin Island was approximately ten to one: ten amputations for every hand gripping a handle.

507

The sea we thought we could see was the sky we thought we could beat.

508

I know the end is coming (the when, the how, the why) but by then I'll alrcady be goue.

509

The final paper on the new-regime entrance exam lasts twenty-seven hours and asks if the Blood Cube glows after a massacre when there's no one alive to witness it glowing.

510

P: Concepts such as good and evil are inappropriate for a

collection of atoms.

G: You're making me nervous.

P: The hell with it.

Z: What are you doing?

P: Preparing for further satanic happenings.

Z: Let's detonate some explosives, get shot out of here forever.

511

They ask if I'm going to report them, and I clear the drug paraphernalia from my desk, and they say we want to eat your head, and I open a tin of old-regime dog food and mix it with the translucent stuff oozing down my legs, and they gobble it up.

512

In the name of the new regime, kiss me like a virus.

513

I don't care if some goons with shotguns come in right now and blow my brains out, because to die between these floorboards would confirm divine intervention.

514

The neo-regime answer to every question was "When the bloodbath blooms flowers."

515

The old-regime's demise was the end, but the resistance remained resisting the new regime.

516

We met at a poolside after-bombing party and talked in gossip-column style about the beds we slept in, the bugs we collected, and the skin we gathered in preparation for the plunge.

517

Yellow autoerotic-asphyxiation suicide backpacks are installed in all post-regime recruitment centers.

518

Resistance slogan (1,984): use blood to brood in a journal before you bleed.

519

These cute and playful parcels flew along odd lines of flight into the new regime.

520

I regret the bloodbath, and the bloodbath regrets me.

521

Goons hanging around in airport bars and business lounges sway conversations until whoever's there oscillates between juvenile drunk and aggravated battery.

522

Whenever the masters of the new regime suggest mass suicide, the lower ranks roll their eyes and continue to rape and murder children.

523

Outside the hospital's sliding glass doors, my body is a mangled trash pile, half dead over there, reaching up a bloody stump, trying to get attention, but the nurse's eyes are focused on the distance, and the cigarette in the nurse's hand is a closed speedboat loop.

524

Old-regime identity divisions (etc.) were designed (divined) to bring about a bloodbath.

525

The only intimate act is cupping a hand around the back of a beloved's neck because we know at any time comes the blood blade and the rape gang.

526

Cracking open skull after skull, and trudging through the sludge, unable to tell ourselves if the thoughts we form in our own skulls are our own thoughts, is what it is, but it is never all.

527

We are either asleep with the pressure of bleeding or awake with the pressure of sleep.

528

These (space)ships were constructed from "bones" beyond human, and they left for lands inhabited by those beyond human (return to return).

529

Post-regime slogan: blood restrains the world.

530

Crows fell from the yellow sky whenever the Blood Cube called us (black rain fog machine).

531

On another channel, there's the heady drift of boiled cabbage and shredded skin, firecrackers exploding through various puzzles, floating corpses in wire cages, and I arrange my clothes in the shape of a body and slump onto the bed.

532

Z: PLEASE COME DOWN AND DECAPITATE ME

because I desperately want to see my head cut off, myself die, it's a thrill for me, the sight of severed heads sends chills up my spine, which is exactly the point, it's not supposed to be painless.

P: You talk too much.

533

The Mad Dream Later was a revolutionary performance-art script conceived by window cleaners broadcasting endless telepathic death-waves across the city.

534

Dropping subliminal messages in antenatal classrooms, the old regime succeeded in grooming unborn babies into believing their calling in life was death by brutal hands.

535

The post-regime regime stepped up toy production, and some of us felt the horror, and some of us felt no more.

536

In the back of a taxi, we unearthed a pain translator (Semax267), the one resembling a radio, but the signal was stuck, and the sound was a long-gone flame.

537

What the Blood Bath said: "For those about to drown, we pollute you."

538

Tapping cigarette ash into an open palm, smooth skin, slender fingers, grimy nails caked with earwax and amphetamines, the taxi driver asked, "Where are you heading?" and we said, "Anywhere not leaving us headless," and a gun slid across the dashboard.

539

The regime's most extreme Atrocities were the ones unrecognized and unrecorded.

540

I expected my neck to leak blood, imagined blood over the tiles, staining the grout, running into the cracks under the walls, but there was no blood, or there was too much.

541

This blood is proxy blood, and this flesh is proxy flesh (ketchup and corpse paint).

542

It's dark of course, midnight, not as though time or light matter, so I shouldn't have mentioned them, and forget I did if it helps, although you probably can't forget, and anyway, I hear a phone ringing, and someone answers it, saying yep, erm, hello.

543

A: What are you doing after this life?
T: People who collect karma are called by many names.
A: What about water?
T: You must be a buffalo.
A: When was the last time you were this apprehensive?
T: At the start of Generation Bloodbath.

544

The visionary producers of *Backpackers Trashed by Axes* lured crowds from their homes for the first time in twenty-seven years by replacing theater carpet and upholstery with plastic and subjecting six random viewers to the same murders happening on screen.

545

Old-regime epigraph: enter the bloodsuckers with their VHS nostalgia dumped in trunks behind suburban car parks across a decommissioned world.

546

Unlike any regime, no one leads the resistance.

547

Blood sacrifice keeps us afloat (speedboat to the stars).

548

Anyway, back to the present.

549

The community of rape dress in matching tracksuits and unused running shoes, and they apply identical makeup and tie back their hair to emphasize their jawbones for the hunt.

550

I pump blood from a dispenser into my mouth and vomit into a bucket.

551

Goons follow me to my apartment and set fire to my children.

552

There is no exact, translatable, regime equivalent for Generation Bloodbath.

553

One problem lies within the assumption that the resistance exists outside our perception of its existence resisting.

554

Post-regime spinoff update (5.5) (episode eight, scene three): on a wall in an office in an abandoned skyscraper hangs a framed reproduction of the elusive Blood Cube.

555

A telephone rings in a darkened room.

PART 666

Symptom of the Universe

Take me through the centuries to supersonic years

Electrifying enemy is drowning in his tears

556

If you're reading this, the obvious has happened, and you've received sufficient details to relieve me of the duty to inform, but I wonder about how they told you, the tone, the body language, the diversions and padding, the light in the interrogation room.

557

Sabotage the insurrection and erect the cocktail bars!

558

The metal riff on *The Mad Dream Later* soundtrack was clearly inspired by an outtake clip of a bar scene from the third season second episode of *The Regime Knows*.

559

The feedback drone rumbles forever after no one's there to hear it.

560

We initially imagined the visitors were vampires (all hail the golden bullets).

561

They broke into motel rooms and smashed TV sets and threw them into bathtubs and spray-painted the walls with Generation Bloodbath.

562

We cajoled them into drinking too much blood (never enough).

563

They joined the death squads to drink the blood of goons hanging around demolished hospitals.

564

The Corpse Rape Initiative (CRI) was more popular than NSI, so live bodies were imported from the colonies, fed a diet of leaves and bark for the three-year trip, and killed on arrival.

565

Old-regime dictum: the compression of intention and technique is the method being executed, the method of execution.

566

Z: Let's nail up posters of people not missing.
P: That's your dumbest idea.
Z: It isn't mine.
G: How about dead people?
Z: What's death?
T: Absence of life.
C: What's absence of life?
T: Reality exposed.
A: Do you have a line to the source?
T: Where shall we nail them?

567

One hack to the spine with a cane machete says more than all works of old-regime literature.

568

Blood fuels the (space)ships.

569

We bought tickets to the midnight roasting and bathed in horse-blood hot springs.

570

What is the taste in our throats if not the live things in the dead things in the live things in the dead things in the backwash of post-regime clarity?

571

Hyper violence came in waves of blood, whole countries gone in a single weekend.

572

One continent faked its own death and collected the insurance (ketchup and corpse paint).

573

Murdering backpackers is old-regime easy.

574

Deep in the woods, the woods are deep.

575

An eye peeks through the cabin door, slightly ajar, muzak playing, tap water running black and heavy, white lights hovering in the sky, white lines dotting the road, the road becoming the sea, the sea becoming the sky, the lights becoming degenerate stars.

576

And we, the blood worms in the dead bodies in these car trunks, in these ship hulls, and in outer space, call upon the new-regime goons to drown in their own blood.

577

G: What are the rules of Generation Bloodbath?
P: There are no rules.
G: Are we there yet?

P: We never left.

Z: It's beautiful.

578

In the beaten church in the shattered village, the donkey-child altarpiece smiles, as if saying the way out is the way in.

579

Hair clumps hacked away, formaldehyde and other smells, unrelated, are all I remember from the first wave of air attacks, but now this memory, the texture or sadness or futility, harbors more horror than the entire bloodbath.

580

If *Backpackers Attacked by Axes* in any way mirrors *A Picnic of Six,* the resemblance has been lost on most pseudo-scholars of the neo regime.

581

We were meant to transport blood, but we drank most of it before we reached the colonies.

582

To call the cities graveyards, and the buildings tombstones, implied the dead were buried, and they were dead.

583

I unclip my stitches, open my stomach, and search for explosives until the floor is a mess.

584

Blood money is the only currency remaining to exchange.

585

We followed the dead-truck highway going south in winter.

586

Our love for the resistance was a transistor radio, held in the hand of an unborn pacifist, or placed on the ledge of a kitchen window, broadcasting unwritten blood songs.

587

In the car park of a demolished shopping mall, a wall of amplifiers emits a subsonic drone.

588

After the virus removed our capacity for empathy, the line between ourselves and others blurred into an infinite bloodbath.

589

A gun going nowhere is the same as a face exploding in reverse (pyrotechnics).

590

The old regime mixed carcinogenic, intramuscular compounds with laundry powder, and our dogs sniffed the air drifting through suburbia, but we pacified them with narcotic snacks.

591

Neo-regime rite: we bleed you in the way of ancient dogs.

592

After-bombing parties screen movie-magic nostalgia (*Backpackers Thrashed by Axes*), and the subtext is about the construction and destruction of bodies and the institutions defining them.

593

I suck and blow the memory of yellow clouds, the smell of

black rain, and the heart-attack coma scars, sprawled on the kitchen tiles, blood dripping from the edge of a dirty spoon.

594

The Anti-Spy X946 is a solar-driven eavesdropping device designed to detect other solar-driven eavesdropping devices within a one-mile radius.

595

From ruin to ruin, we wandered through firebombed cities abandoned to botulism.

596

The sign above the entrance to this bloodbath recital hall demands cutting off your tongue eighteen seconds before entering (let the blood spray guide unsteady footfall).

597

"I'm nervous," I said, meaning I was terrified.

598

At least we were buried in our battle jackets and Generation Bloodbath T-shirts.

599

T: Let me feel it with your hand.
A: Sure. Yes. You can feel it.
T: Do you love me?
C: Is this related to the escape plan?
T: Dump your tattoos and don't be a snitch.

600

The phone kept ringing, but there was no one on either end.

601

Our lives were plural before their grammar jammed us.

602

The dynamite rammed down our throats burns less than the words they forced us to speak.

603

On a break between lectures, I sit under a tree and eat a sandwich and stare at the yellow sky some say used to be blue.

604

Regime proof = anti-regime (and so, here return the blankets; my mattress a bloodbath of space junk all the way to the stars).

605

It was at a poolside after-bombing party, and I was wearing a kidskin mask, and I don't remember much about the party or the mask, but there was a murder show, and some cryptic messages appeared in the midnight sky.

606

Keep the customers alive.

607

The children of the night market are comfort-zone rejects (jet packs for suicide belts).

608

As an educational tool, Blood Screen (Extreme Youth) facilitated institutional eradication, but anyone who survived the program became a wasted, gibbering, freakshow pencil pusher convinced these times were the end times.

609

I was standing in a classroom on the first day of new-regime elementary school, and the tears were coming, and my legs were bleeding, and outside was snowing, but I threw a flowerpot through a window and escaped to join the resistance.

610

Scratch marks in plasterboard forewarn me as I enter another six-month spell in another deadbeat motel, and I figure I'll be dead before I dig a pathway out.

611

The blood stains on the bathroom mirror resemble Earth maps before the flooding.

612

Another crucial difference between the neo regime and the new regime was the focus on deliberately bastardized simulation rather than inherent obsolescence, but the showers remain.

613

I crawl from the cave into a shopping mall.

614

The freedom we sought when our names and countries were erased came back to bite off our hands.

615

I talked to butterflies and tasted rainbows (it was not how it was).

616

The knives we knelt before told us about the sound of death.

617

We were squinting at the writing on the table, all these gory notebooks.

618

The post-regime resistance anti-mantra is so complicated to articulate, both in manner and place, it leaves reciters choking on their tongues.

619

Jetlagged, bored, neurotic (six backpackers arrive on Severin Island).

620

My room sits upstairs, three steps broken, banister wobbling, and it collapses, and I fall.

621

P: If I inject you with this, you won't feel any pain.
Z: I don't want it to be painless, I want it to be REAL, I want it to STOP, a bloodbath judgment for my years of insane reading, and I can only ease my irritation when I'm holding a knife or spinning scissors or kissing a pistol.

622

Eat graffiti: the virus ran its course, and the world evolved into chaos.

623

The end of signs was the end of love.

624

Canonical zombie texts of the old regime depict corpses searching for the reproductive organs of other corpses, a representation of what they say life was before the regimes.

625

Six old-regime blankets are preserved in unknown locations in intricately decorated sutra boxes.

626

Shelter from the new regime meant cannibal feasts in shopping malls heavily cursed by their own metaphorical emptiness.

627

With the distinction between snuff and special effects a distant memory, the neo-regime's media industry consisted entirely of nostalgic splatter films modelled after *Backpackers Trashed by Axes*.

628

Post-regime execution parades escalated to such an unprecedented level, linguistic teams were employed to rename these and other new spheres of horror.

629

Mopping blood from hospital floors has not occurred since the early days when there were hospitals and when blood was an abundant commodity.

630

If we learned one lesson from the resistance, the lesson we learned was taught to us in an old-regime dialect, and the journals we were forced to compose contained less life than autopsy photographs, but reading between the lines was a death sentence.

631

A disembodied voice desperate to speak on the other end of an unanswered phone, in the place of damaged organs, is trying to say, "Sugar poison, terminal honesty, scary love."

632

We sewed up their lips to quieten the begging, and we shot them in their hands, which were covering their eyes, to distort the signs.

633

Under the new regime, the only sexual prohibitions (consent, age, sex, gender, animal, human, living, dead, visitor, other, etc.) were the ones we never articulated.

634

Incapable of providing pleasure, the children of the night market were utilized for providing table space, trash boxes, and toilet bowls.

635

The Fetish Nightclub sign on the elevator led to the wrong floor, an empty corridor, an empty view from an empty window, an airplane in the distance, fingerprints and skyscrapers dripping in blood.

636

I smashed the glass like a page or a screen or some other kind of post-regime junk.

637

To call us cannibals implies the flesh we eat is the flesh we are, but vampires escape the distinction with their random bloodsucking ways.

638

Destroy the Face (DF) Stab Project (42): maximum disfiguration + minimum medical treatment = escape from human form (cage of sanity).

639

Blood Yoga torture failed to counter double-agent resistance on the astral plane.

640

I drag on my boots in the dark, dust off a coat belonging to no one alive, and stumble through the shattered shopping mall.

641

The spaces between vehicles narrows rolling down a dirt track, and a tank drags itself through dust in the opposite direction, and the sun's shining through layers of yellow sky, and backbones are jutting out at different angles from chunks of dry and cracked bone-field mud.

642

Metastasized from weeds, a drive-in screen appears like the sail from a shipwreck.

643

New regime: Where are you?
Old regime: Where are you?
Neo regime: Where are you?
Resistance: Where are you?
Language: Where are you?
Formula: Where are you?

644

Because in retrospect our time spent with the resistance is so romantic, the blood pumping from our torsos is a gift.

645

None of us ever stepped foot on a beach before the sand was red.

646

Autopsy journals written on Severin Island were confiscated and believed burnt, but shaking haze amnesia, as with any predictable plot involving stateless people consuming street medicine, left a single copy in a suitcase buried in a coastal cave.

647

I roll on my side and write a poem on the back of a coffee cup.

648

Above my face, or a face I used to call my own, before space travel and forensic science downgraded us, some wrists are tied together, legs spread, armpits curved, a ribcage and chest bone, but the noise coming from below deck chills me more than this suspended vision.

649

A green balloon floats on a string tied to a bed frame in a demolished hospital.

650

We offered our organs to the new regime, and they said they needed more blood.

651

The lies we tell ourselves are the lies we've been told to tell.

652

A drain in the interrogation room was the only ever exit.

653

Another regime is another resistance.

654

A: The goons must take it out somewhere.

T: They're trained in torture methods.

C: On the deck this morning, I saw a robin. It bounced across the bench I was resting on, and it perched for a time on my bucket.

T: Did it make a noise?

C: It made me cry.

A: I remember seeing this on TV.

655

A swinging wine bottle shatters my face, and I'm back blinking into the headlights.

656

I wrap the steering wheel to my wrists and ram the truck over a security goon at the end of the pier, and a hacksaw desert opens out beyond the page.

657

The words we use are never as precise as two shots to the head, and in there lies their beauty.

658

How to Fuel the Speedboats (101): stand over a bathtub, slit your wrists, and drink the blood (the moment you collapse will be captured in your own mind, and for us you will live forever).

659

I stick the knife in my abdomen (real hard), and I'll never forget the sound, never forget the sight, at first clean and white, then shot full of sapphire before the blood comes sloshing.

660

Suicide paradox (94): the nightmares you are trying to escape evaporate the moment you kick off the chair.

661

A tail disappears behind the curtain, and a face in the mirror comes into focus, but never gets there, somehow slightly gone, and the failure of both, the tail and the face, reveals more than the usual lifestyle tips promoted in post-regime junk mail.

662

Our existence was different to the lives depicted in new-regime literature (their blood was paper cuts; marginal, and ours turned the pages back to pulp; a corpse field of guillotines).

663

In the final scene of *Backpackers Trashed by Axes*, the final girl floats on a raft in an ocean of blood and broken glass and glances back at Severin Island to see several mangled metal objects in a clearing, a rudder covered in weeds, a fuselage wedged between two rocks.

664

Ex-regime memory (13): we knew the resistance would win.

665

The last sound on Earth was the Blood Cube buzzing.

666

In the field with empty carcass, we sit with both eyes broken.

AFTERMATH

TV-FUZZ illuminates the strip under the restroom door and I feel it glimmer and shift as I search for escape instructions in the toilet tank telling me to thread a belt around my neck hooked up to a towel rack and for a second opinion I consult torture rhythms from the faucet because earlier the pipes around here were running water instead of blood and the rhythms say no chance you're sticking this one out so I count on my radio to break the deadlock but it refuses to get involved and I shake it and replace the batteries and take it apart but when I reassemble it the speaker remains silent so I crack the plastic shield over the destination numbers and the tuning dial swings a red needle here and there across empty space and next I remember I kept the tennis ball you rolled up your leg and over yourself the first time we met by the swimming pool at an after-bombing party in a hotel converted into a hospital and you were hilarious and I loved your poems hung out for the package to arrive on weekends in a romantic montage scene of anticipation with stock photos set to music featuring me sitting in dappled sunshine on a brownstone doorstep smoking a cigarette and listening to my radio and reading a pulp thriller paperback and chatting with neighbors about the apocalypse while ignoring their convoluted conspiracy theories and whatever-regime platitudes never considering you would set me up or double-cross me and not considering your poems might be the last lines of our language but vaguely imagining it would be cool if they were and more concerned about you and the resistance you and the revolution you and the goons building cages around your decommissioned apartment locking you in dismantling the place brick by brick substituting your medicine for vitamins until you were ready to jump and the kid you somehow found as a body double and when they figured you were missing I tried to strangle you because you told me it was hopeless but I couldn't do it because your eyes spoke of alternatives so we stole a battered car with a speedboat engine running on blood the engine backfiring around corners until we arrived at an empty swimming pool in an old brick building with a glass pyramid roof and we made our hideout in a vacant changing cubicle and you told me you wished your sibling was here crumpled up burned rotting under the bench and it made me cry and it makes me cry now as I exit the bathroom and in the TV light I see your amputated hand I failed to reanimate crawling through syringes and broken glass across the floorboards and organs floating in formaldehyde jars on the desk and I brush aside all these other failed experiments the loose-leaf papers covered in blood and scribbles and put on some head-phones and listen to my heartbeat and the clock on the shelf until it becomes the knocking on the door and when I open the door a rogue goon from a backwards local chapter of whatever regime says *the game's up you're coming with us* and the goon punches me in the stomach and breaks a couple of ribs but I can't feel it because I'm already high on gutter coke and plot anticipation and I get in enough stabs and slashes to sever the arteries and the lines be-tween pronoun and flesh fade out and after draining enough fuel from the goon's neck for a two-day drive I hit the road thinking of you and the tennis ball on the dashboard and your poems those dejected episodes delivered like electric shocks or viral implants in similar cool nights in dead-channel TV light with friends sitting around a table listening and clapping and when the power failed for good I taught you how to play the drums and we made a rack-et in the desert without concern for the goons banging and screaming until our hands bled and our arms throbbed and our screams reached a point where they were silent but when I was waiting for you to get discharged from the clinic I looked for signs on the pink walls covered with posters of dead rock stars and ac-tors and the cat curled up on your lap and you couldn't say a word or make a sound from the triangle above the bed because your tongue was too gone hacked out after your sibling's burial cere-mony and your arms were anemic blood sloshing through biceps hanging there belonging to nobody and at a traffic light on the trip back to your apartment someone leaned in the side window shouting *long live the whatever regime* and stabbed the taxi driver in the head and the taxi driver continued driving until the stabber slipped away and we watched the summer heat and terminal boredom fuel further acts of random violence where people went out looking for a good time and ended up raping or murdering visitors or being raped or murdered themselves or each or both and other cliches from this toxic state-sponsored roadkill paralysis some blamed on the virus or the media or the politicians or the people or the economy or the environment or asteroids and degenerate stars tilting the Earth's axis and others blamed on the visitors because they couldn't or wouldn't talk back in approved languages and you told me in a poem because you couldn't talk anymore *the truth is misleading there's usually another angle but if you always wanted to kill someone or yourself moral and ethical considerations are meaningless and we should do it together because now we are siblings of our own bodies* so we decided to flip a coin heads we're gone tails it's a visitor but by the time the coin landed we were already knee-deep in a bloodbath and you told me you knew the world was fucked when you woke up to hear mumbling gibberish from a voodoo ritual in a zombie movie and you found a severed head in the toilet and the pipes ran blood and the drains backed up to flood the apartment with blood and cleaning it up took several days and never truly dried and was the worse experience of your life at the time and this was before you lost your sibling and we lost our sense of time all calendars adjusted in conformity with trials beyond our control happening in the woods the mountains the people the horses the goats the grotesque rituals and satanic sacrifices and our sense of sense and no matter how low those early days became they were only the surface wave of incoming horrors and if I dwell on later horrors they become more real and more traumatic and it's selfishly as much to do with losing you as it is with losing our languages or ourselves and the world being gone so right now I've been driving all night and my brain's exhausted from brooding over you and the world and how it all relates to me in the end and I'm swerving across what's left of this bombed and decommissioned highway but I make it to a dirt track running alongside the mess of blackened trees in bloody fields and from there I eventually pull back to a steady pace and cruise as much as cruising is possible in this rickety vehicle and there's this tinkling music playing in my head and I pass through a village in confluence a town in oblivion a hilly area bombed into a valley and I reach the tributary of a blood lake encoded with human genes merging with a boat ramp and leading into the darkness and I park the car by a speedboat crashed on the lake's edge and I check out the speedboat but it's a self-fueling model without a tank the siphon hooked up to the dead driver's neck the tank empty and I rip off my stinking clothes and burn them for firewood and I refresh my bruised body in the lake while watching city lights flicker in the distance and I consider taking the dead driver's clothes but they're in a worse condition than the ones I burned and I don't uncover other equipment worth taking but I rip the pipes from the speedboat engine and the driver's neck in case of an emergency and later on before the city's suburban out-skirts I stop at a mansion with a black tiled entrance giving way to an open-plan lounge dining room kitchen with exposed beams jutting from the ceiling to the floor to indicate where one section ends and another begins and in the kitchen area a steel refrigera-tor and dishwasher stand open and in the dining area a glass table holds a napkin pinched into a triangle a silver platter and two wine glasses and under the table lies a mess of human torsos bloated and watery random chunks missing rolled in chicken wire crisscross patterns and I uncork an apparently excellent bottle of red wine and drink it in one go and continue creeping around for new clothes or valuables but there's nothing much on the ground floor except memory-lag projections of ghostly servant figures squatting in open doorways some eating rice from bowls balanced on their fingertips and others scrubbing dishes in plastic buckets wedged between their thighs and I take the stairs slowly weary of goons down the hallway decorated with family portraits and in a bedroom a dead kid who was in several photos now has his head caved in with bits of brain and skull hanging out sitting slumped in an ergonomic study chair in the plastic wrapping and I discover a blood-soaked rag doll sprawled across a blood-soaked pillow and I dab the doll's legs on a computer keyboard until the screen flashes on before going black for about twenty seconds followed by numbers and letters scrolling down while the motor grinds its cogs and the cooling fan splutters and the motor dies and I drag some clothes from a drawer and put them on and then I collapse on the bed into instant sleep and my dreams merge with the dreams of the dead kid at the keyboard studying for an unpassable whatever-regime entrance exam dreams about being outside the mansion searching for a pet dog and greeting the dog and playing fetch with the dog with your tennis ball looping through the chill morning air before landing in overgrown grass and racing to retrieve the ball first and rolling with the dog in the overgrown grass until being called inside to eat rainbow cereal and blast whatever-regime zombie video games mirroring what the world became when the world first ended when burning apartments and office blocks collapsed in pungent winds from visitor attacks and occupants became trapped in basement shelters overcrowded after arrivals of inhabitants from other buildings or other worlds rendered unsafe and many occupants perished from heatstroke and carbon monoxide poisoning and many more drowned in bloodbath sewers and after siphoning enough blood from the dead kid for a few extra hours on the road when I leave the mansion the sun's a blood sphere coming up in the dead kid's dream fresh calmness and I can't hear any tinkling music but in the rearview mirror I glimpse an execution plantation with children impaled on the same stakes as their parents' stakes not sharpened too much otherwise the victims could have died of shock before they died of agony and bleeding out or so the theory goes bodies left on stakes for months organized into geometric patterns and when I look back at the dash your tennis ball's gone so I climb out the car and trudge through the execution plantation my eyes half closed cautious in case there's a goon lurking behind the meticulous arrangement of corpses the bamboo torture statues but I can't find your tennis ball in the spot where I imagine it landed in the dream I shared with the dead kid and it could be a different area but it's tough because the grass is gone so I stumble down some steps carved from the plateau and bordered by logs where I spot your tennis ball in a puddle of gore and as I bend to pick it up my body shudders with some kind of brain spark my hands twitching involuntarily and when I regain regular consciousness I'm back in the car on the dirt track running alongside the decommissioned highway where I'm wearing the clothes from the dead kid in the abandoned mansion and your tennis balls sits bloody but secure wedged between the dash and the windshield guarding the car and guiding the way but the city center lies further in the distance than it was before and I can feel in my bones the black rain coming and I hope the trunk seal holds to keep the trunk dry but in case it's a brutal storm I unspool the last gaff tape which helped dampen my drums and I add a final layer of reinforcement and now there's nothing I can do except push onward into the clouds hovering over the outer suburbs and my stomach feels gross and I don't want to eat because it's probably the amphetamines I scraped from the dead kid's desk or more wine from downstairs me tasting the wine and the wine tasting of blood in my memory but I don't remember storing the taste of blood in my memory because all I remember is you too many tears sweet life words whispered dissolving between the dawn loneliness a kind of silence or a beautiful insanity and so on for example you stopped writing and looked at my hands because I was wearing surgical gloves way too big for me and I had no shirt on naked above the waist and the pen lid scratching under your neck was a helicopter and we were so stoned we joked about the goons returning and we were drinking the next day but soon ran out of beer and you took a left turn too fast and overcorrected yourself and crashed the driver's side into a palm tree killing you instantly on impact and me coming away with some kind of brain damage stumbling around an arch of corroded railroad tracks driven vertically into the ground to form a swimming enclosure with shorter pieces as crossbeams and a wire mesh cover for rejecting sharks and jellyfish but not stray tentacles or sea lice which itch me now in my memory the tide lapping out twenty-five meters past the enclosure plastic bottles and shopping bags floating in bloody pools around the base railroad tracks reclaimed slaughter lands subdivided into plots marketed as a village with bikeways BBQ areas swimming pools an open graveyard church carved from a clearing bodies distorted and attached to the Earth's exhaust mechanisms in slanted towers some teeth coming loose so I spat them out and looked left into the sun over a dirt track leading to a whatever-regime training ground and I thought of giving up and joining the other side or it was different and you turned right and crashed into an oncoming truck killing you instantly on impact and me coming away with a different kind of brain damage or I was driving and you were in the passenger seat and as we turned left a speedboat came over the bloodbath waves and crashed into the passenger door killing you instantly on impact and shunting us sideways up the gutter and into a pizzeria and me coming away with some other kind of brain damage and me following the pizzeria owner who made a U-turn into my lane and I went for the brake but changed my mind because it was the owner's child and I wanted to see what would happen the speedboat's front end crumpling and the radiator bursting all trauma remained whatever with kidney and liver disease and brain surgery in a makeshift hospital with gangrene amputation and clothes for firewood but in truth it's all such a blur I have no idea about any other subject than an infinitely collapsing mouse without skeletal muscles all hardship and shame and wasted possibility making conscious understanding impossible *you see the mouse* and now a fresh hallucination happens inside my breakdown pain shutting off actuality too far gone no fear of death no flatline narrative no consistent or coherent or cohesive way to spin the web and no chance of being recruited by whatever regime but I recover somehow my skull and friendly faces from the resistance who'll also remember you and idolize you and who worship you in a platonic or romantic rather than a political or religious sense converse with my limbs through massage gestures unexpected and methodological and somehow this kept me going not out of nostalgia but respect or neglect or indifference or negation of a freedom referring to itself and how if they ask if a bloodbath remains the same we must say no and if they ask if the bloodbath changes with time we must say no and if they ask if the bloodbath is at rest we must say no and if they ask if the bloodbath is in motion we must say no because such answers must be provided when interrogated by the goons of whatever regime about any condition because they're making a zombie cannibal movie with the walls rolling repeatedly and sleepwalk translations and gut reading texts and I remember you being obsessed with selecting and preparing the language and images you produced through processes of correction and condensation and organization and other modifications because it was how you approached life and love and art and cinema and the way you stroked my hair and flipped the camera upside down and wiped the blood from my face and from the camera and you turned around and you looked at me and you grinned at me and you rubbed your eyes and when you were panting or yawning or glancing away from the camera an echo in my mind never fading continues to play your miraculously reborn voice saying *I can teach you how to come back from disappearance* and you probably have most ingredients somewhere around your apartment or we can go to the supermarket because yes it was the same morning we wanted to get more beer wearing sports coats and baggy trousers tied with electrical cords to hide our weapons and you search my pockets before we leave playing goons interrogating each other and falling laughing on the bed where you discover two coins and a space probe and I pretend to be a visitor spinning satanic trash talk and making ridiculous faces and holding my breath because I don't need oxygen and for a moment you believe me but I'm choking and the space probe is a fake space probe made of aluminum foil and toilet roll or not a fake space probe but a hallucination of a fake space probe and the fake space probe hallucination is wet with blood and it crumples into a ball in my hand and I'm coughing into the crumpled bloody ball in my hand and the crumpled bloody ball is the tennis ball on the dashboard your tennis ball and there's nothing in my hand except the steering wheel I'm gripping more tightly than babies huddled from bombs in bloodbath fields grind their teeth and your tennis ball's safe on the dashboard and I can smell the rain although it's not here yet and it might not fall or tears are destroying my eyes because I'm reminded of babies and about when I found out after the crash I was pregnant and you were dead and I didn't know what to do because I had no idea how to raise a baby and by then most of your friends had been killed or vanished so far underground I couldn't contact them but I couldn't let go of our baby of course partly a selfish way to keep you near and bipolar obstacles battled inside my head and I was determined to see it through but those disgusting creepy goons in animal suits goats and dogs and donkeys and also birds and reptiles eagles and snakes and I'm not sure how many but into double figures and anyway they found me and fooled around with me for a while pushing and slapping me because they were searching for you and your poems or your voice of dissent and they didn't believe you were dead forcing a gun in my mouth and yelling *he's alive and you're lying but when he comes back you'll be dead and we'll be laughing* and they filmed this ridiculous pseudo-ritual with your camera because they said it was your eyes watching them rape me and they were jostling for position no way choreographed porn instead going for any hole they could enter with themselves and their guns and they figured out or already knew I was pregnant and they pulled it out with coat hangers and pliers and a box cutter in my guts for fun as a climax to the ritual the whole place a bloodbath and they were hooting drunk and calling me all kinds of dumb shit I couldn't follow about the fetus being an alien creature or a demonic insemination from a cheap horror movie and how they were tossing it back and forth a bunch of jocks with a football spouting jokes about halting an evil lineage and somehow getting hard over this ridiculous situation and I was out of my mind with my mouth taped shut and out of my head with my body tied down but also floating above the bed and viewing the scene and I'll never comprehend how it could turn them on because the fetus was dead and the blood and placenta were splattered on the white walls and they were licking it and eating it and wiping it on themselves but it was of course more about anger and hatred and humiliation and retaliation and retribution and ugliness and power rather than erotic or perverted love or lust and they weren't into it but they wanted to show each other they were into it and how you used to talk about some people being born with particular attractions such as for a doorknob or a horse or a young child or a rotting corpse and how all of those could be love beyond our ability to judge but this was nothing to do with love a frat boy fear party with the fetus playing the role of unspoken object dividing or creating a barrier between their individual desires and I knew our baby was already dead but they were getting cheap thrills from making me watch them trying to fuck the fetus and playing a bukkake fetus game high-fiving each other when they were done and afterwards mashing the fetus into a bloody pulp and kicking and punching me until I blacked out and a few days later came around in a gutter in a pile of dead bodies and decapitated and disfigured and otherwise discarded bodies and body parts some fresh and others rotting the protagonist in a grindhouse exploitation revenge film but I didn't want revenge because I knew I would never track them down and anyway it would be the same as biting back a dog that bit your hand unaware of what it was doing and not excusing them wondering would they do this if they were alone and someone found me and no matter how many times I've been raped there's usually one who has this stance saying *it's the others and not me and I'm only doing this because they told me to and don't stare at me like that I'm different and if this situation was different and it was me and you it would be cool and romantic and we could go on a date to a movie or dinner or drinks* and those ones are actually the worst ones because they have some kind of conscience or conception of decency but they're too feeble to use it when their buddies are around so it's on with the show and I was back in another makeshift hospital praying the attack never happened and I was never pregnant and I was in hospital after the car crash but I knew it was real because they left the camera on the bed and the bloodstains on the walls and their conviction you were alive nearly made me believe you could have survived the car crash and I knew you didn't survive because I held you when your heart stopped beating and I hacked off parts of you in the hope of reanimating you but although they smashed up the apartment they never found you or your poems and now the tinkling music is back in my head but it's a different loopy bossa nova and the car's coming into the outer suburbs scattered with demolished office blocks and apartment buildings and a paper construction factory and a subway station crossing a shredded street and it feels easy to get lost in this metaphorical journey across a godless universe drifting through an unrelenting text not as a mystery to be solved or puzzled out but as a visceral flyover bypassing the narrative grid and the facade of story and going straight for the mainline to the organs or the nervous system or into the city's heart or head to decapitate the capital and on the left sits a substantially damaged graveyard shopping mall probably protected by goons and abandoned tanks and missile launchers in the car park and a ray of sunlight comes broken in a scattered line across the windshield and I mistake the ray for a target aimed at blowing off my head and I'm pondering the immense ruinous promise I made to you to remain sane whatever sanity means before returning to dust and one set of traffic lights on the road blinks orange and some kind of canal advances zigzagging into the distance and I reach the edge of a bridge crossing the canal and I'm shielding my eyes from the sun but expecting an explosion because the bridge is standing and the gravel has been graded but the canal is littered with landmine robots and the road on the far side is smoother recently resurfaced and this way means trouble but it's also probably the fastest way to the source and although I don't have any evidence and don't believe it's true I was apparently part of a special project attached with a codename used for experimenting with pregnant visitors because homemade medication and non-existence meditation can impress anyone at first glance on the astral plane and the Earth is heavy but the sky is heavier and we are already in space and the leaders of our present fuckhead empire yesterday or today or tomorrow thirst for agony toward visitors but how we exist here is a consolation prize consolidated from condensation and the king lunatics will continue discharging carnage as a formality with flamethrowers tested for survival extinction until this soundwave invasion reaches its apex stacked and shaken as a rolling wave of earthworms and at this point the city is already typecast with larvae complexes churned out flowing a sickness memory future washed gleaming and a breakneck hypnosis of nothing much at all but rotting human flesh ripped apart in cannibal playgrounds and cruel songs and roaming murder sex-doll motorcycle gangs and air-conditioned earthquake simulation and rape-game TV poems and allergic magazine stands and virus vending machines and the glittering shadow trail of counter-revolutionaries cracked between supermarket doorways and I shake these images from my head and try to concentrate on the road because I almost ploughed into a ditch and I feel my mind is rapidly degenerating into a language swamp and this scares me more than being shot in the head by a sniper or stabbed in the heart by a goon and I ease off my foot wrapped too tight around the accelerator and I hold a straight line and take each bend on the brake and the tinkling sound is getting louder coming from the rear speakers or the holes cut in the ledge above the back seat where the speakers sit wafting blood fumes from the gas pipes and soon a truck overloaded with dead bodies washed up on the beach and drained white from fueling speedboats appears behind my car and it's a beautiful afternoon and along the road crawls a mixture of rusty tractor frames and motorcycle engines welded together and they ignore me and all traces of negative antimatter are momentarily removed and my feet are cool and covered in mud and I sit up straight and glance around for the sake of glancing around on a suburban excursion and some parts have been flattened and other parts have been rebuilt identical houses and occasional playgrounds and schools and churches and community centers spreading across the bloodbath flatlands without grass or trees and as the density of buildings increases the clouds cover the sun and soon there's black rain pelting with crows and the traffic is backed up leading into downtown but either some fuel was stolen when I was sleeping in the mansion or the engine's malfunctioning so I unravel the speedboat pipes and jab the syphon hook into my neck and the pain reminds me of my recurring dream of stabbing you where I lash out from some vague frustration and immediately pull back and you appear sad and disappointed to have witnessed this ugliness because of course you've done nothing to deserve it and I'm shocked and embarrassed to have exposed my ugliness so I stab you more viciously to cover up the initial wound to wipe out your recognition and the thought of you holding onto this ugly moment and my wrist jars as the knife chips bone and sometimes it's another botched suicide attempt and it's near water or it's a car job or it's a rooftop and you come back after you're dead and I have to hide in an office block until you die and waiting there I'm in a speedboat drifting further and further away from the shore and I didn't realize I was in a fucking speedboat and whenever I told you about the dream or spent time showing you the presence of toxins or pathogens in our food and medicine you joked about getting a restraining order from the goons of whatever regime and each moment in my memory or in your poems a turn of phrase or image or instruction or tick or action has profound exuding meaning on many different levels and increasingly I dreamed the aftermath without the murder but it's the same murder action scene from the same murder action dream because I've had this dream multiple times before but this time it's real and although no one's found out I can't live with accepting someone might one day and I wake up multiple times within the dream gasping my life is now fucked and I miss you too much and I wish I'd thought about

living more in those days and all I want is to go back and for life
to turn out better or differently and you'd remind me how life was
fucked before we met and life was fucked after we met and life will
remain fucked after we've left and in there lies the beauty and *is
that why we met* but you never believed in destiny and anyway we
wouldn't have met if life wasn't fucked and we might have vanished more quickly if life was less fucked and you'd also add some-
day when I've swallowed enough I'll possibly flip the placebo and
join them but you had a timid glint in your eyes and a goofy smirk
on your face and your legs were slightly buckled from riding horses in the mountains when you were young and your abnormal
gait eventually ruined your tennis career and the tinkling music is
drowned out by the noise of downtown streets barricaded around
the space center with armored vehicles and electric fences and
missile launchers and acid vats and fire walls and fireworks and
fog machines and I close my eyes the moment I'm certain I made
it in time to see the last spaceships depart and a weight floats from
my chest and my muscles relax and a gigantic screen is playing a
countdown superimposed over a documentary about the space
bureau's glorious achievements and the new worlds' endless won-
ders and the car can barely move so I watch the show and I watch
the crowd watching the show although they'll never get to the new
worlds and most have given up trying to scramble aboard the
spaceships or been burned back by flamethrowers or gunned
down by death squads or crushed by tanks or choked by leather
boots and smoke bombs or strangled in barbwire and now on
stage a heavy metal band is playing a sinister riff louder than the
crowd and as the drums come in I'm taken back to being in the
desert with you when our hands could feel to grip the sticks and
our screams could conjure poetry from the void and on stage
snuff-pop idols are being raped and executed as a final blood sacrifice to the universe for a safe flight for the spaceships and the
screen shows similar satanic scenes of sexual slaughter in stadiums
and concert halls and dive bars left standing throughout the world
and I've experienced this all before in a midnight movie we all

laughed at before the world went mad but if it's possible to verify memory it presumes learning marks the brain carrying information through time and objects such as a speedboat circuit or some other conceptual contraption extracting empty experience from touch and the circulation of blood through the heart and the cerebral-arterial circle supplying blood to the blood vessels in the neck and head and brain and the car won't move anymore spluttering out near the mountain of decapitation and the slaughter-fuel processing plant and I blow a kiss to the dashboard and your tennis ball glows before it disappears and I rip off the blood pipes and run through the traffic jam to the N-gram Sky Tower and judging the departure schedule by the rumbling first I locate a hidden washroom in a state of speechless cleanliness and I unearth a buckled faucet and cool liquid runs through a few fingers my hands making a cup full and overflowing and I bring the cupped handful of water up to meet my face as it stoops to meet the handful of cupped water and I splash my face alert and run wet hands through my hair to flatten it as best I can and then I'm dodging around goons who are more interested in assaulting each other than stopping me and I'm taking the stairs two at a time and halfway up I'm dizzy and nauseous and hyperventilating but I keep going until reaching the top floor and I regulate my breathing enough to maintain focus and I wander down a hallway to an office with a view and inside the office I rip the venetian blinds off the windows and through the black rain falling I see the launch pads opening at the space center and the sound vibrates through the building an epic earthquake tremor expanding up the magnitude scale until it feels impossible to get any louder but it keeps getting louder and objects are falling light fixtures and ceiling fans and air vents and bookcases and filing cabinets and I'm crying and laughing and I'm covering my ears for a while and I'm holding onto a desk for a while and I'm trying to keep standing and the noise not only continues to escalate but also merges with some other sound the slurping drone of a billion speedboat engines draining seven bloodbath seas and it comes to an unbearable crescendo rupturing physical reality before the spaceships take off in an earsplitting crack of light and the cacophony drops away and the stillness and serenity and silence replacing the noise and light are unfathomably dark and infinitely deep and my ears are buzzing or it's the tinkling music from the car but it isn't my ears or the music it's a phone ringing across the office and in the shadows a prosthetic hand picks up the phone and the ringing stops when a finger presses a button those two actions don't match up and have been spliced together and when the phone is next to a hearing aid a voice says *this is not what you want to hear but I'm going to talk it anyway and you're going to hear it and the words you hear will be different from the words I talk* and then another voice says *this is not what's happening here* and another voice is shouting *shut the fuck up and sit down you spoiled snotty little cunt or I'll shoot you right where you stand and I might do it anyway because god knows you have it coming right down to the cellular level* and out in the regularly scheduled universe the sound of tinkling and buzzing and telephones has merged with sirens and fire alarms and earthquake warnings and hordes of confused and disoriented goons having lost their link to the central narrative or been decapitated and turned into zombies are roaming the smokey hallways and I hit the stairway three steps at a time rattling the banister and choking on the fumes and halfway down twisting my ankle into a feral limp and slowing progress to find the foyer crowded with rogue goons on fire and I dodge into the hidden washroom and search for escape instructions in the toilet tank telling me to thread a belt around my neck hooked up to a towel rack and for a second opinion I consult torture rhythms from the faucet because earlier the pipes around here were running water instead of blood and the rhythms say no chance you're sticking this one out so I head down a deserted corridor and bang open an emergency exit into an alleyway littered with dead bodies cannibalized and drained or ripped apart by other bodies many who've died while trying to feed themselves slumped with amputated limbs or infant torsos in their mouths and I'm coughing smoke until my lungs are clear and I'm breathing more easily out here with my hands on my head and above the city's shattered neon and beaten architecture there's no more black rain because the spaceships have scattered the black crows but the yellow sky's dark because the sun's given up on us repulsed by the spaceships or busy doing lighting on another show and after turning back from a dead-end fence I exit the alley into an open square formerly swarming with cafe culture now an ancient ruin disregarded by everyone apart from several kids in corpse paint and ketchup stains squatting and searching in the rubble and when they notice me they scan me like I'm a visitor so I give them a half-smile that comes off more threatening than uncertain and I kneel in the rubble and pretend to pick up your tennis ball and pretend to serve your tennis ball gently underarm to them and a couple of them track it looping through the air and one moves to catch it but after the first, second, third bounce, the world explodes.

INDEX

Part 111 (Black Sabbath)

1. New-regime iconography

2. Cannibal trains

3. Headless pity

4. Regime influence

5. Indie reports

6. Perfect picnic spot

7. Knife writing

8. Regime advertising

9. New-regime art

10. Old-regime cereal

11. Dialogue 1: Take them away.

12. Resistance slogans (mirror shards)

13. Ship's galley

14. Last new-regime class

15. New-regime hatred

16. Blood barn

17. New-regime wounds

18. Postmortem interviews

19. Home Invasion Therapy (HIT)

20. Fleet on fire

21. Old-regime novels

22. Dialogue 2: We love you.

23. Knife angles

24. Tanks are back

25. Distorted voices

26. New-resistance interview

27. New-regime devices

28. Old-regime DNA

29. Psychedelic bloodbath (neo-regime)

30. Headless hallways

31. "Human Square"

32. Endless imitation

33. Old-regime T-shirts

34. Haunting the new regime

35. Impending extermination

36. N-gram Sky Tower

37. Words for water

38. Sleeping barn

39. Post-regime life

40. Frantically drunk

41. Snow-globe shipwrecked

42. TV-FUZZ

43. Last dispatch

44. Dialogue 3: Are you coming with me?

45. Wall of light (pyrotechnics)

46. The end of time

47. Resistance manifesto

48. Drunken space wreck

49. Cinema hallway

50. Schools undemolished

51. Neo-regime orphanages

52. Unending tunnels

53. Pharmaceutical detectives

54. No pleasure

55. Speedboat visions

56. Visitor suitcase

57. TV-FUZZ tagline

58. A Picnic of Six

59. Slaughterhouse flowers

60. Head

61. Bloody sediment

62. Old-regime proverb (hammer)

63. Telepathic blood transfusion

64. Blood-soaked notebook

65. Rope

66. Dialogue 4: Stop. Wait there. Come back.

67. Telescope (time machine)

68. Our sincerity

69. The last to leave

70. Counting the dead

71. Old-regime ghouls

72. Necro Solar Intercourse (NSI)

73. Blood balloons

74. Photo evidence

75. Radio birds

76. New-regime souvenirs

77. Airport drone (truck)

78. White van

79. Shatter

80. Hotel room ("Violent Sleep")

81. Undercover agents

82. The gods

83. Rape play

84. Unconfirmed reports

85. Poison

86. Backpackers Trashed by Axes \ (original)

87. What the Blood Bath said (hang)

88. Dialogue 5: Have you ever been in love?

89. The dead leader's donkey-child

90. New Regime Year Zero

91. Vanished cities

92. Cinema knives

93. Beyond the knives

94. New Regime Intergalactic Headquarters (NRIH)

95. Bomb craters

96. The ships set sail

97. Weekend retreat

98. Fire walk

99. Dialogue 6: Are we dead as well?

100. Dear X

101. New-regime entrance exam

102. Snuff Corpus Atrocity

103. Old-regime dreams

104. Burial T-shirts (resistance)

105. Endless bloody churn (black rain)

106. In the cabin

107. Cult bullies

108. New-regime memory (74)

109. New-regime phone call

110. Rabbit cave

111. Early days

Part 222 (War Pigs)

112. St. Regime

113. Infect the planet (visitors)

114. Travel adaptor

115. New-regime nonexistence

116. Blood sting

117. Training hall

118. Murder dreams

119. End of civilization

120. Satanic graphics

121. Generation Bloodbath T-shirt

122. Dialogue 7: Keep a record of what happens...

123. Mechanical typewriter

124. Neither/nor

125. A knife to the neck

126. Words on the back of your thigh

127. City burning

128. New-regime nostalgia

129. Cut, cut, cut

130. Spaceship rats

131. River's edge

132. Anti-resistance protesters

133. Dialogue 8: Can't we talk this over?

134. Degenerate Stars

135. Assassination simulation

136. The trip of writing

137. Graffiti bridge

138. A hammer in the face (88)

139. Taste

140. Old-regime linguistics

141. Old-regime comeback

142. Amputating hands

143. Neo-regime iconography

144. Resistance origin story

145. Blood Red River

146. Terminal K

147. The taps

148. Blood highway (crumbling lines)

149. Unfold the map

150. The way life never was

151. Elevator shaft

152. Impostor syndrome

153. Backpackers Trashed by Axes (premise)

154. Any good movie

155. Dialogue 9: What are the rules...?

156. A speck of madness

157. Resistance slogans (blood loss)

158. Absolute revolution

159. Violent sleep

160. Overpass

161. Digital Deluxe Death Watch

162. Forget

163. Physiology

164. Heal

165. Old-regime answer

166. Speedboat to the stars

167. Backpackers Attacked by Axes (opening shot)

168. Wheelchair precipice

169. Gasoline cigarette

170. Sacred chant

171. Corpse waste

172. Golden path

173. Space bait

174. The Blood Licking Wall

175. Blame the visitors

Part 333 (Into the Void)

Part 444 (Snowblind)

345. Torture porn (outer space)

346. Satanic leeches

347. Resistance mantra (1,914)

348. Collision-dowse button

349. Strangulation robots

350. Corpse paint cooked by the sun

351. If not for the blood

352. Brain mechanics

353. Exiting the city

354. Spent shell

355. Dialogue 20: If someone wrote a book...?

356. Desert drone (crater)

357. Dig the vampires

358. Ecstasy

359. Pre-regime memory (18)

360. State of bovinity

361. Snow globe

362. Golden column

363. Bloodbath Sea (simulated sun)

364. The bloodbath you take

365. Cramped suburban hell

366. Millions marched

367. A darker exit

368. Despite being broken

369. Neo-regime proverb (limb)

370. Blood addiction

371. The forest

372. Karaoke town

373. Four months later

374. Boiling plasma

375. Fog machines at dawn

376. Fuel the spaceships

377. Dialogue 21: I don't want to cut you anymore.

378. Virtual Mutiny Visualization (VMV)

379. Blood Yoga

380. Resistance tattoo

381. Cheapest trick

382. The taste of my mouth

383. After three days

384. The movement of blood

385. In the squalor

386. Space travel

387. All hail the golden bullets

388. Taxi driver

389. Nothing is everything

390. Shattered TV

391. Old-regime virus

392. Karmic Verdict (39)

393. Congratulations

394. A junky's delicate ritual

395. Clarity (old regime)

396. Backpackers Attacked by Axes (TV series)

397. New-regime logic (shopping carts)

398. Dragnet corpses

399. Dialogue 22: Generation Bloodbath will...

400. Post-regime foreplay

401. Posthumous self-pregnancy

402. Night bus (yellow clouds)

Part 555 (Sabbath Bloody Sabbath)

457. Deflated balloons

458. Suicide note

459. Sleep paralysis

460. Burial T-shirt (stains)

461. Speechless

462. Lunchtime bar

463. Lesser conclusions (violent sleep)

464. Sending in the dogs

465. Plastic straw (night market)

466. Dialogue 26: I don't know what they're talking...

467. New-regime passport photo

468. Oxygen is overrated

469. Between the commercials

470. Medical practice

471. Alternative Communication System (ACS)

472. Hollow books

473. The last linguistic turn

474. The blood kept us indoors

475. Acid River

476. The old planet

477. Clogged

478. Moist overdose

479. The sound of flames

480. Birdsong

481. Fake bloodbath (ketchup and corpse paint)

482. Clockwork world

483. Neo-regime radio update (356)

484. Medicinal fix

485. Cauterized organs

486. Backpackers Trashed by Axes (integrity)

487. If you burn alive

488. Dialogue 27: Why didn't you answer the phone?

489. Being undercover (counter agent click track)

490. Napalm

491. New-regime internship

492. This is real

493. Auto-fuel speedboats

494. Child steaks

495. New Regime Award for Literature

496. Velocity

497. After grammar

498. The surface

499. Impossible rebirth

500. Less alive

501. The radio

502. Backpackers Attacked by Axes (trauma)

503. Autopsy journal

504. Blood blisters

505. Flashback (45)

506. Cane-machete ratio (Severin Island)

507. The sea

508. I know the end

509. Blood Cube (final paper)

510. Dialogue 28: Concepts such as good and evil...

511. Translucent stuff

512. Kiss me like a virus (new regime)

513. Divine intervention

514. Neo-regime answer

515. Old-regime's demise

516. After-bombing party (plunge)

517. Suicide backpacks (yellow)

518. Resistance slogan (1,984)

519. Odd lines

520. Bloodbath regret

521. Airport bars

522. Mass suicide

523. Trash pile

524. Old-regime identity divisions

525. The only intimate act

526. Skull after skull

527. Sleep

528. (Space)ships

529. Post-regime slogan (blood)

530. Blood Cube (black rain fog machine)

531. On another channel

532. Dialogue 29: PLEASE COME DOWN...

533. The Mad Dream Later

534. Death by brutal hands

535. Toy production (post-regime regime)

536. Pain translator (Semax267)

537. What the Blood Bath said (drown)

538. Headless

539. Extreme Atrocities (regime)

540. Blood leak blood

541. Proxy blood (ketchup and corpse paint)

542. Midnight phone

543. Dialogue 30: What are you doing after this life?

544. Backpackers Trashed by Axes (gimmick)

545. Old-regime epigraph (VHS)

546. Unlike any regime (resistance)

547. Blood sacrifice (speedboat to the stars)

548. Anyway

549. Community of rape

550. Blood dispenser

551. Apartment fire (goons)

552. Generation Bloodbath (translation)

553. Existence resisting

554. Post-regime spinoff update (5.5)

555. A telephone rings

Part 666 (Symptom of the Universe)

556. Relieve me of the duty

557. Sabotage the insurrection

558. Metal riff

559. Feedback drone

560. Visitors were vampires

561. Generation Bloodbath (motel)

562. Never enough

563. Death squads

564. Corpse Rape Initiative (CRI)

565. Old-regime dictum (compression)

566. Dialogue 31: Let's nail up posters of people...

567. Old-regime literature

568. Blood fuel

569. Midnight roasting

570. Post-regime clarity

571. Hyper violence

572. Insurance (ketchup and corpse paint)

573. Old-regime easy (backpackers)

574. Deep in the woods

575. Cabin door

576. Blood worms

577. Dialogue 32: What are the rules...?

578. Donkey-child altarpiece

579. First wave of air attacks

580. Backpackers Attacked by Axes (scholars)

581. Transport blood

582. Dead and buried

583. Explosives

584. Blood money

585. Dead-truck highway

586. Blood songs (resistance)

587. Mall drone (car park)

588. Infinite bloodbath

589. A gun going nowhere (pyrotechnics)

590. Intramuscular compounds

591. Neo-regime rite (ancient dogs)

592. Backpackers Thrashed by Axes (subtext)

593. Dirty spoon

594. Anti-Spy X946

595. Ruin to ruin

596. Bloodbath recital hall

597. Nervous

598. Battle jackets (Generation Bloodbath)

599. Dialogue 33: Let me feel it with your hands.

600. The phone kept ringing

601. Plural

602. Dynamite

603. Between lectures

604. Regime proof

605. After-bombing party (kidskin mask)

606. Customers

607. Children of the night market

608. Blood Screen (Extreme Youth)

609. New-regime elementary school

610. Scratch marks

611. Blood stains

612. Another crucial difference

613. Shopping mall

614. Freedom

615. Butterflies and rainbows

616. Sound of death

617. Gory notebooks

618. Anti-mantra

619. Jetlagged (Severin Island)

620. My room

621. Dialogue 34: If I inject you with this...

622. Eat graffiti

623. End of signs

624. Zombie texts (old regime)

625. Old-regime blankets (sutra boxes)

626. Cannibal feasts

627. Backpackers Thrashed by Axes (neo-regime)

628. Execution parades (post regime)

629. Mopping blood

630. Death sentence (old regime)

631. A disembodied voice

632. Distort the signs

633. Under the new regime

634. Table space

635. Blood window

636. Post-regime junk

637. To call us cannibals

638. Destroy the Face (DF) Stab Project (42)

639. Blood Yoga torture

640. No one alive (shopping mall)

641. Bone-field mud (yellow sky)

642. Shipwreck

643. Dialogue 35: Where are you?

644. Gift (resistance)

645. Sand

646. Autopsy journals (Severin Island)

647. Coffee cup (poem)

648. Suspended vision

649. Green balloon

650. More blood

651. Lies

652. The only ever exit

653. Another regime (resistance)

654. Dialogue 36: The goons must take it out...

655. Swinging wine bottle

656. Hacksaw desert

657. The words we use

658. How to Fuel the Speedboats (101)

659. Sapphire

660. Suicide paradox (94)

661. Behind the curtain

662. Corpse field of guillotines

663. Backpackers Trashed by Axes (final scene)

664. Ex-regime memory (13)

665. Last sound on Earth (Blood Cube)

666. Empty carcass

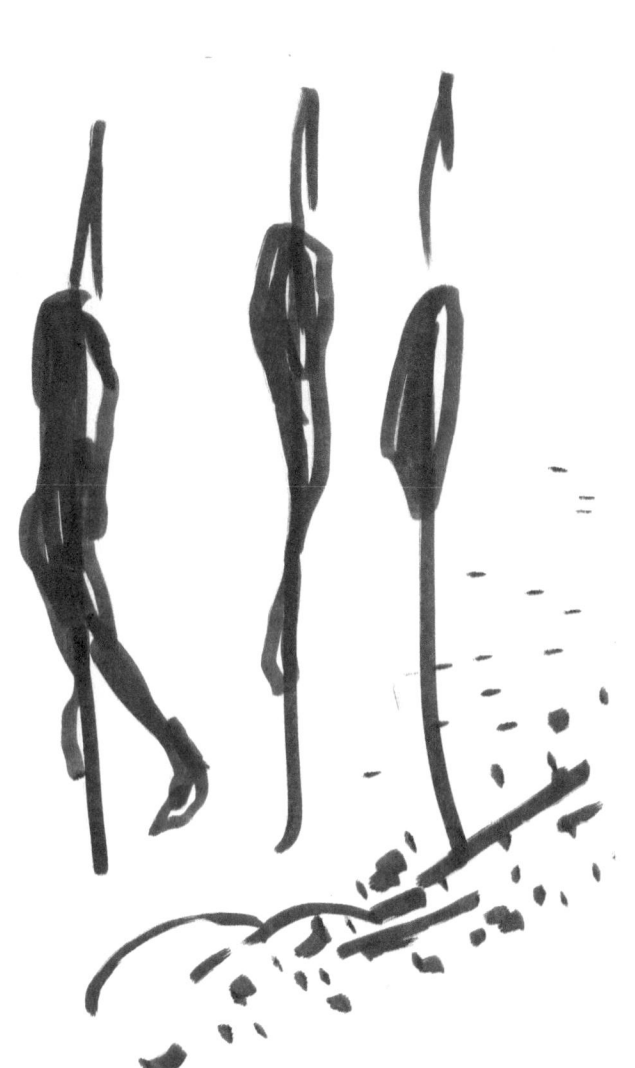

Paul Curran was born in England, grew up in Australia, and lives in Japan. As a teenager, he played drums in heavy metal and alternative bands before switching to guitar as a founding member of Gravel Samwidge. His previous book is *Left Hand*. Other recent writing has appeared on SELFFUCK and in the Infinity Land Press Anthology. He's currently writing a book about the Setagaya Murders.